pasta wars

ELISA LORELLO

pasta wars

A NOVEL

ADAPTIVE BOOKS

AN IMPRINT OF ADAPTIVE STUDIOS
CULVER CITY, CA

For my grandparents, Mary and Biagio Mottola,
who taught me the secret ingredient in every aspect of life.

Visit us on the web at www.adaptivestudios.com

Library of Congress cataloging-in-publication number: 2015960616
ISBN 978-0-9964887-5-4
Ebook ISBN 978-0-9964887-8-5

Printed in the USA.
Interior design by Neuwirth & Associates

Adaptive Books
3578 Hayden Avenue, Suite 6
Culver City, CA 90232

10 9 8 7 6 5 4 3 2 1

one

There are two kinds of people in this world: those who love coconut and those who hate coconut. I am not one of the coconut people. In fact, I happen to think coconut is the work of the devil. Think about it—would a benevolent deity invent something that could cause brain damage if it happened to fall on your head from a tree? Would it grow on trees in the first place? Would its innards be shaved and shredded into a confetti-like substance that could double as packing filler? Would it get stuck in your teeth for days? Weeks? *Months*? Like, you go to the dentist, and she crinkles her nose and furrows her brow and digs that torture hook between your incisors, muttering to herself, "*What IS that?*" Oh, it's just coconut from a cupcake you ate in 1992.

I mean, it tastes good and all, but so not worth the effort. Give me Nutella on a graham cracker. Give me chicken marsala. Give me red velvet *anything*.

Don't even get me started on coconut water.

In a span of three days, coconut managed to ruin my life.

I'd just returned home to Long Island from the *Food & Wine* Festival in Miami, entered the house calling out for Max, abandoned my coat, overnight suitcase, and briefcase by the door, and headed straight for the barren kitchen. It's a habit—open the refrigerator door after a long flight or stressful day at work, stare at its inhabitants in wistful longing, and close the door—I don't even do it consciously anymore. There's not much in there, usually, save for plastic baggies of carrot and celery sticks, salad, a pitcher of cucumber-infused water, and at least one half-empty bottle of chablis. The freezer, on the other hand, is jammed with an assortment of Pasta Pronto meals. Since founding the company nine years ago, I'd made it a leading contender with Lean Cuisine and every other weight-loss line in the frozen food section. "Carbs for the Calorie-Conscious" is our slogan, coupled with our mission statement of "Lite Indulgences for Women on the Go." Last year we rolled out the new Slimline Spaghetti series, and we exceeded sales projections months ahead of schedule.

My eyes honed in on the Styrofoam container sitting on the top shelf, and I peeked inside.

Breaded coconut shrimp. Odd. Max is allergic to shellfish.

"Honey?" I called from the kitchen. No answer. I went to the garage entrance to see if Max's car was still there. It was. He moved into my house when we got engaged six months ago, and the sight of his car in my garage—*our* garage—still made my heart flutter with sprinkles. Like finding the perfect frame to a photograph. Proof that you really can have it all, if you want it badly enough.

I returned to the showroom-style living room—designer sofa and loveseat; apothecary table; lamps from a specialty store; custom plush carpeting—and leaned on the staircase banister. "Maaaaaaaaxxxxxx?" I called again, with a more seductive tone this time, my voice echoing. "Come out, come out, wherever you are . . ."

Seconds later, I heard the bedroom door open. Max jolted down the stairs. "Katie! Hey, honey-muffin," he said. He leaned in to kiss me on the cheek and pulled away before I had a chance to nuzzle against his sandpapery beard or clasp my hands around his neck. What gives?

"Where's the fire?" I asked.

He headed for the kitchen, looking over his shoulder at me as he spoke. "How was your trip? I wasn't expecting you home until tomorrow."

I scoffed as I followed him. "These events are getting so snooty. Pasta Pronto sells, like, five times more product than these vendors, and they're all like, 'oooh, oooh, frozen dinners aren't *food*'!"

"Jealous, babe," said Max. "No one makes a better fettuccine alfredo than you."

"Especially at three hundred calories!"

"And in three minutes."

"EXACTLY."

He looked as if he'd just come from the gym. Chestnut hair tousled. Pupils dilated. Sweaty.

"You okay?" I asked.

"I'm fine," he said, averting his gray eyes at the last nanosecond. "Why?"

"You buttoned your shirt wrong."

He jerked as if someone had snuck up on him from behind and given him the Vulcan nerve pinch. "Shit!" he exclaimed as he frantically realigned the buttons. "I . . . I didn't even notice. To think I've been walking around like that all day."

"Bad day at work?"

"Meh. The usual. Cuppiecake, why don't we skip nuking the noodles tonight and go out to dinner instead? Say, Francine's? We haven't been there in ages."

I shook my head and went back to the fridge, with Max seemingly vigilant of my every move. "Can't," I said. "I was totally Code Orange this week. My avatar went up three dress sizes!"

In addition to the meals, Pasta Pronto had its own weight management system, complete with a food journal app in which you created your own avatar, and color-coded food rankings: Green was "safe," Yellow was "good in moderation," Orange was "danger zone," and Red was "nuclear meltdown." When you entered your food intake in the journal (you're allotted as many Greens as you want per day, three Yellows per day, one Orange per day, and only one Red per week), the size of your avatar adjusted according to your portion and food selection. If you wanted something simpler than color-coding, you could also scan a food nutrition label in the supermarket and an angel or devil icon would appear. The app was a huge hit with our customers.

I retrieved a baggie of celery sticks (Code Green) from the fridge and plopped them on the food scale. Then I pulled half of them out and returned the baggie to its place. "This will have to do. By the way, cinnabun, whose coconut shrimp is that?" I asked, pointing to the container.

4

Max stared at it as if he'd never seen it before. As if he'd never seen the inside of a refrigerator, ever.

"It's mine," he said, sounding uncertain.

"Yours? Are these magic shrimp? Hive-free?"

He backpedaled. "The restaurant must've given me the wrong doggie bag." Now he seemed even more doubtful.

"Which restaurant?"

"A bunch of us from the office went out to lunch today."

"And you want to go out again for dinner?"

I heard a door close lightly, as if trying to go undetected, and my ears perked up like a Jack Russell terrier's as I whisked around.

"What was that?" I asked.

"What was what?"

"A door closed. In this house. The front door, to be precise."

"You're imagining things, Katie."

"You know very well I am not imagining things." Max told people that I would be able to hear footsteps on the moon.

And then it all conglomerated into one gooey, globby mess: the coconut shrimp. The disheveled shirt. The evasive kiss on the cheek. The befuddled tone since I walked in the door. *I wasn't expecting you until tomorrow . . .*

No.

No, no.

No-no-no-no-no.

I broke into a dash for the staircase, tripping on the third riser as I tried to pull off my pumps along the way, and could smell the foreign fragrance with every step. Was practically assaulted with it, like when soda gets caught as you swallow and goes up your nose instead.

"Sweetness, wait!" Max called right behind me, scaling the stairs two risers at a time. I froze in the bedroom doorway and took in the scene:

The Hotel Collection sheets and duvet: tangled.

The Sterns and Foster pillows: head imprints. One on each pillow.

The corner bedpost: shackled in handcuffs.

And *OH MY GOD, WAS THAT A PILE OF BUTTERFINGER WRAPPERS ON THE FLOOR BY THE FOOT OF THE BED???*

Max's and my engagement portrait lay facedown on the night table—I wondered: was it knocked over during the sex, or did they think they were doing me a favor by hiding two-dimensional-me from the scene?

The sex? Holy frappe, *the sex????*

"I-I-I'm sorry, Katie. I'm so sorry."

His hand on the back of my shoulder felt like a slab of ice.

"You . . . ? Here . . . ? Wha . . . ?"

I turned to face him. He looked like a kid who'd just been caught with his dad's *Playboy*.

"Who?" I asked.

"Who, what?" he responded.

I could push him down the stairs, right now. One little shove and this would all be over.

"*Who?*" I snarled.

He gave in. "Cheetah," he said as he stared at his socks.

Cheetah? Cheetah, the Hostess with the Most-ess from the Cheesecake Factory—*that* Cheetah? My high school *nemesis*? Also the work of the devil?

That was her actual name, by the way. She beat me out of the Entrepreneurs Club contest with a caramel apple moon pie recipe that she stole from a *Woman's Day* magazine. She drew mustaches all over my student body president campaign posters. She stole the box of brownies I'd made for Kyle Carney on Valentine's Day and presented them to him herself.

"She's never had an original idea in her life! She says things like 'O-M-G.' She . . . she makes *hourly*!"

"She also *eats*, Katie."

"I eat plenty," I insisted.

Shit. That totally didn't come out right.

"I mean, she eats *real* food. It's not her enemy, like it is for you. Lately I've been finding that very . . . well, appetizing."

Real food. I could've maimed him with a coconut at that moment. After I set fire to my bedroom.

two

I still couldn't believe it happened.

One minute my fiancé's car was in my garage. The next minute not only was his car gone, but also everything else of his. Plus he was no longer my fiancé. Thanks to Cheetah once again taking what was rightfully mine.

I made Max move his things out the very next day—anything left behind was dumped in the trash. Told him to take the bed with him as well, and I ordered a new mattress the same day, sleeping in the guest room in the meantime. In the time it took two movers to transport Max's foosball table from the basement-turned-man-cave to the truck, I ate my weight in Mallomars. (Red Alert! Red Alert!) And I'd been *so good* maintaining my size two for the wedding. *No way* would I accept alterations unless they were to take the dress *in* rather than out. I was going to fit into that Vera Wang gown if I had to go down the aisle on an elliptical.

Ugh.

No wonder he cheated on me. My avatar looked like Santa Claus in a dress.

Mallomars. Almost as evil as coconut.

Never mind that I held a bachelor's degree in management and an MBA. Never mind that I singlehandedly taught myself the ins and outs of starting and running a food company, my own frozen pasta product line, and even basic chemistry. Never mind that I'd won awards in leadership, marketing, and the best low-calorie food for your buck.

Who was I kidding? I was going to have to sell the house. Everywhere I turned, a memory of Max's and my almost-two-year relationship lurked in a corner or behind a photo or between the cushions.

The painting of the coastline that we bought in Amalfi to celebrate our engagement.

The time we tried to make s'mores in the living room fireplace and accidentally burned a baseball-sized hole in the carpet straight through to the floor.

The sex on the kitchen floor. And in the shower. And on the couch in the den. And on the dining room table after everyone left on Thanksgiving Day last year. Okay, so sometimes I needed to schedule it along with my spin class and hot yoga, and nothing kills spontaneity more than *Siri, remind me to have sex with Max at 9 p.m. tonight*, but still. Max was punctual.

The *abruptness* devastated me more than anything else. One minute Max and I were blissfully in love, complementing each other like spaghetti and meatballs, and the next minute we were . . . *nothing*. We were a plate of neglected food dumped into the trash. No more love notes. No more two o'clock texts.

No more couch-cuddles. No more spooning in bed. No more pet names. It ended in the blink of an eye. Made every part of my body hurt.

You know when you toss and turn for seven hours, and then you fall fast asleep ten minutes before your alarm goes off? In that morning's case, day two of Max being gone and day one on the new mattress and sheets, the ringing smartphone on the bedside table jolted me upright. The beauty blindfold still shading my eyes, I slid it off and squinted to stave off the assault of sunlight peaking through the window treatments as I felt around for the phone. I accidentally pushed it onto the floor—thank God for carpeting. Seconds before the call was about to switch to voice mail, I slid a finger across the screen without looking at it and spat out a groggy "Hello?" while still hanging off the side of the bed, my arms dangling to the floor.

"Miss Cravens, it's Evan Goldberg."

That name should mean something to me.

"Evan?"

"Evan from Quality Control . . ."

I pulled myself up to an upright position. "Oh! Right! Evan! Sorry, I was sound asleep and I haven't fully woken up yet." I peered at the clock. *4:48 a.m.? This can't be good.* "What's wrong?"

"The message boards have lit up. The recent shipment of coconut chicken on orzo dinners—you know, from the 'Or-Zo Yummy' line—people from all over the country ended up in the ER after consumption. Stomach pains, diarrhea, abnormal vomiting . . ."

Was there such a thing as *normal* vomiting? If so, then what distinguished normal vomiting from abnormal vomiting?

I rubbed my eyes and sat up at the edge of the bed, digging my toes into the carpet.

"Oh, lordy."

"It's bad, Katie."

My stomach lurched. "Please, *please* tell me there weren't any deaths."

"None so far, thank God."

I exhaled an anxiety-ridden sigh of relief.

"What the hell caused this?"

"We're trying to find out. I've issued the product recall, and not just for the coconut chicken. They've all got to go. Everything should be off the shelves already. And I updated the website with the symptoms and set up an 800 number to report cases."

"The lawsuits . . . my God, the lawsuits. Evan, HOW IN GOD'S NAME DID THIS HAPPEN?"

"We're investigating."

If I didn't know any better, I would've thought maybe Max somehow slipped a little battery acid into a vat. Or maybe Cheetah did.

Get a grip, Katie. This is your company. Your baby. Your LIFE.

"When you find out who's responsible, don't just fire them. *Ruin* them. Do you understand me?"

"Got it," said Evan. "You need to make a statement. You can't hide from this. Get to HQ in an hour for a press conference. Can you do that?"

"I'll be there," I said.

The culprit turned out to be one of the preservatives used during the freezing process that produced an adverse chemical reaction to the recently upgraded plastic covering for the dishes. Regardless, the damage was done. Within hours of the product recall's breaking news on CNN, a class action suit was filed against Pasta Pronto. Production ground to a halt. To make matters worse, food reporter Meghan Martin released ingredient lists of all Pasta Pronto foods, and claimed that very little food was in them. Social media lit up with a barrage of complaints on the Pasta Pronto Facebook page, trending hashtags on Twitter, and the message board comments on our official website got so ugly at one point we shut the board down completely. And of course, every story was more sensationalized than the next. Pasta Pronto was comedy fodder for every talk show, food critic, and celebrity chef from coast to coast. Mario Batali dubbed us *Pasta Povera* (*povera* translated as *poor* in Italian), along with the even more depressing *Pasta Passata* (*departed*), implying its imminent doom.

Once the legalese was all sorted out, I knew what the result would be: Pasta Pronto—*finito*.

My fiancé was gone. My business on the verge of destruction. My credibility ruined.

Coconut = evil.

three

I spent the next six months doing damage control—not only with the company, but also with the demise of Max and me. Both had consumed my days and nights without a break. I canceled the caterer and the cake and the flowers and fired the photographer and lost my deposit on the reception hall and informed the guests that the wedding was off and deleted every photo of us from my phone. I tried to cancel our honeymoon to Bermuda, but Max, the cheating, cheap bastard, insisted on keeping it. To go with Cheetah. Offered to reimburse half of it, but still. And what woman wants to go to her boyfriend's former honeymoon destination?

On paper, Max was reduced to nothing but a story that had ended abruptly. In my head, however, he was a living, breathing character who betrayed me and broke my heart with every Butterfinger and coconut shrimp that crossed my path. Not that I ever let on. No, on the surface I was Katie Cravens In Control. I had always been cool under pressure. And I did my best to avoid his haunts in the city—we never did much on Long Island except the occasional dining out or staycation in the Hamptons—and dreaded the day I might actually run into him or the friends that had come with Max as a package deal when we'd started dating, my own friends sinking deeper into the recesses of we-have-to-get-together-but-never-do that had begun when I'd formed my company.

At the Pasta Pronto headquarters in the heart of Manhattan ("HQ," as I commonly referred to it), we'd documented every food poisoning case, coordinated with our legal team, re-called every single product and reformulated the new packaging. Our crisis management team issued press release after press release and goodwill ads, appeased stockholders, and overall worked around the clock to restore the credibility of the Pasta Pronto brand. Our PR team did the same with social media, offering coupons and giveaways and changing the conversation.

We'd come a long way and made significant progress. Our customers were returning. Our stock value, however, had dropped and remained in a holding pattern, which made us vulnerable. Plus, after the lawsuit settlements, we were in a crunch for capital. I consulted my team for ideas, and the proposed solution came at the hands of Pasta Pronto's Vice President of Product Development, Bill Crumb, who had recently taken a vacation across Italy, with Genoa being one of the cities he visited.

A collaboration. With renowned pasta chef Gianluca Caramelli and his twin sister, Luciana, head of the Caramelli family restaurant and company in Genoa. The siblings were heir to the Caramelli fortune and celebrities in the European food world.

At best, I was skeptical. At worst, I was downright opposed.

We sat around the oval executive conference table cluttered with coffee travel mugs and file folders and computer tablets and a platter of untouched bagels, croissants, and Danish.

"You have to do it, Miss Cravens," said Bill. "If you don't, Pasta Pronto will go in the red."

"We solved the packaging problems, we did the goodwill campaign, we settled the lawsuits . . . I don't see why we have to do a merger," I said.

"It's not a merger, it's a partnership of sorts. A specialty line of gourmet pasta dishes."

"And not a single one of them three hundred calories or less. How does that jive with our mission statement? How does that serve our loyal clientele who rely on us for their weight management?"

"Think of it as expanding your customer base rather than losing your loyal followers," said Evan Goldberg. "Pasta Pronto won't just be 'diet food' anymore—it'll be about good living. And the Caramellis are world-renowned for their pasta cuisine and expertise. This is a win-win."

"Then why did Gianluca Caramelli go on the record saying he opposes the deal?" I asked, having done a preemptive Internet search prior to the meeting. "I quote: 'It goes against everything I stand for.' That doesn't sound like a win-win to me."

"You won't even have to deal with him," said Robert Taylor, VP of Marketing. "Last we heard, he's busy with some Jamie Oliver–type fresh food crusade. His sister, Luciana, handles all the family's business, and she loves the idea. Plus she's a sweetheart. Speaks fluent English too."

"Since when do you care what other people think?" said Wendy Blount, who headed the public relations team and coordinated with Robert as well as the crisis management team. "You defied the skeptics who said pasta couldn't be delicious, fast, *and* calorie-friendly. You also defied the critics who said Pasta Pronto wouldn't recover from the product recall. Despite everything that's happened, you're still in the game. This will keep you there. We'll make sure of it."

One of the strawberry Danish was blaring at me like a blinking red light, and the familiar pang of hunger twitched and squirmed as my stomach gurgled.

Whose idiot idea was it to put out the white flour fest anyway?

Oh. Right. Mine.

I sipped my latte minus the whipped cream (Code Yellow). My advisors were right—I never backed down just because a few food snobs wanted to deprive me of my pleasure. Nor did I give anyone the satisfaction of seeing me suffer. So my company took a huge hit. So Max humiliated me by cheating on me in my bed with a woman who once admitted to backing her car to the foot of her driveway to retrieve her mail rather than walking to the mailbox. I was still getting up at 5 a.m. to do my elliptical workout. My wedding dress still fit. (Okay, so I kept it. And I occasionally still tried it on. I should tell Siri to remind me to stop doing that.)

Not to mention our stock price rose at the mere rumor of the collaboration with the Caramellis.

When the stove blows up, toast marshmallows over the fire. That was my motto.

Besides, maybe it would be fun to go into business with another woman. I was done with men for a while.

four

There are two kinds of people in this world: those who can eat a five-course meal three times a day and not gain an ounce, and those who need to get on a treadmill after merely watching *Guy's Big Bite*. I despise the former kind of people, and resent being one of the latter. Okay, fine. I exaggerate. I mean, yeah, I know the freedom eaters had no role in their DNA or whatever it is that makes their metabolism so efficient. And some of them are as conscientious as I am about exercise and food choice—it's not like they're pigging out on chips and ice cream all day. Perhaps the real difference is that they don't seem to spend as much time *thinking* about food—and the visual consequences of it on the body—as I do. Or *caring*. I've made it my business to be thinking and caring about it—literally—but sometimes I'd like to know what life is like on the other side.

Then again, maybe I don't.

In the following weeks, Luciana and I exchanged count-less emails and phone calls and we were both eager to begin our new product line of haute cuisine. "A Taste of Genoa," we decided to call it. Of course we still had details to iron out, such as what kinds of dishes we'd provide, how to package and market them, and how to make them three hundred calories or less (I was holding out hope for that one). But if Luciana Caramelli, granddaughter of Vincenzo Caramelli and co-heir to the Caramelli fortune, was as smart and sensible in person as she was on the phone and in email, then I was certain she would be agreeable.

Her twin brother, Gianluca, however, was another story. Since the official press release announcing the collaboration, he'd issued another statement emphasizing that he played no role in the deal, called Pasta Pronto "microwave bastardiza-tion" (I wonder how that sounded in Italian. Was there even a word for "bastardization"?), and referred to the venture as "a disgrace to the Caramelli name."

I bet he used Ragu when no one was looking.

That said, Gianluca Caramelli was pretty hot. That classic Italian, olive-toned skin. Coarse, dark hair, curled at the ends. Obsidian eyes. Sculpted physique. One of the eat-everything-gain-nothing people.

"So, we have a little problem," Luciana said at the beginning of our phone call.

In my line of work, problems were never "little."

"Because my brother co-owns the family business and the Caramelli name as a brand, he has to cosign the contracts in order for us to proceed. And, as you know, he's not been as supportive as I."

To put it mildly.

"How on earth are you going to get him to sign?" I asked.

"I'm not sure. He's not been returning my calls. I think we're going to have to ambush him in Alba."

"We?"

"Rosa and me."

Rosa was her assistant, I'd learned.

"Where's Alba?" I asked.

"About a hundred and fifty kilometers from here. It's a small city. He's helping a friend with what you would probably call a 'farm-to-table' restaurant."

My brain lit up with an idea. "Luciana, how about *I* come to Genoa and convince him myself? That way he can meet me in person, see I'm not some monster out to destroy the culinary world, and I can personally convince him to get on board."

"You don't know my twin brother. He's very stubborn. But I would love to meet you in person and show you Caramelli's restaurant."

Stubborn? I once shoved six Starbursts in my mouth after my high school English teacher tried to confiscate them. I'd show him stubborn. And I didn't need Starbursts to do it. Or any food, for that matter.

"Then it's settled," I said. "I'll fly to Italy next week and we'll take care of business there."

Aside from the long flight and the jet lag, I wasn't complaining about making the trip. My staff assured me that the change of scenery would be good, that my fourteen-hour days at Pasta Pronto HQ since the Coconut Calamity were taking its toll. Bags under my eyes. Hair breakage. Neck pain. At least I was back to eating my Pasta Pronto meals. Following the recall, my lawyers had forced me to throw out every last dinner in my freezer. I'd missed them almost as much as I missed Max's neck massages. Pasta had always been comfort food to me. On a rainy Saturday, Mom would fix us Spaghetti-Os. When I was stressed out for finals, fettuccine alfredo was my go-to. When I was sick in bed, egg noodles in chicken broth soothed my aches and pains. Best breakup food? Why, mac and cheese, of course. The cheesier, the better.

But nothing beat good ol' spaghetti and meatballs. Mom always bought the meatballs premade, but the mere smell of them simmering in tomato sauce (she preferred Hunt's from the can) warmed me from the inside out. Smother the spaghetti with parmesan cheese and, well, you've pretty much won at life.

Thing is, my jeans found all that pasta way less comforting than I did. The mission of Pasta Pronto had always been for women to have their pasta and eat it too rather than compromise on their comfort. In the days following Max's departure, I'd needed all the comfort I could get, and couldn't turn to my usual Pasta Pronto staples—Slimline Spaghetti Suprema, Ravishing Ravioli, and Bow-Tie Bowl with snap peas, sun-dried tomatoes, and lemon vinaigrette. Following my Mallomars binge, I was especially vigilant. I'd managed to stay away from pasta altogether and got my avatar (and myself) back into an acceptable size. But comfort? I splurged on an even fluffier, body-burying duvet and butter-soft, astronomical thread-count sheet set for the new bed rather than anything ingestible.

Luciana's assistant, Rosa, who looked like she could easily sustain a career as a runway model—my God, those legs never ended—greeted me in the terminal and, after we retrieved my luggage, escorted me to the town car waiting to take us to the Caramelli family villa in Genoa, where Luciana had invited me to stay.

I mistakenly expected to see more of the coastal flair of Amalfi as we drove to the Caramelli villa. Genoa, however, seemed to have turned its back on the Mediterranean, and not just via geographical location. It paled in comparison, looking more industrial, despite possessing that old-world Italian charm.

"Luci is eager to hear your feedback regarding Caramelli's. She recently made some changes there," said Rosa. Her English was almost as fluent as Luciana's. "New head chef. New menu. They had five restaurants—the original here in Genoa, open for over fifty years, plus Rome, London, Boston, and New York, going back about five to ten years. All but the original have since closed."

"It's got quite a reputation," I said. I'd researched the Caramelli business as well as the family. Critics concluded that although Gianluca Caramelli was "a genius" as a chef, especially when it came to all things pasta, he had no head for business and that's why the restaurants closed and Luciana took over. Rumor was that they were hurting for capital even more than Pasta Pronto was. And although Luciana neither confirmed nor denied the rumor, she hinted that the financial gains of our collaboration would be beneficial.

Rosa continued, "The changes include some 'tourist-friendly' options, much to Luca's objection. It seems to have helped with revenue. But with Luca out of the picture now, it's hard to say what the outcome will be. Caramelli's without Luca is almost as hard to accept as it was when Vincenzo passed, rest his soul."

"Luca?" I asked.

"Gianluca, Luci's twin brother. You didn't know? He's been in Alba for the last month."

"Yes, I do know that. But what do you mean 'out of the picture'? He's left the family business for good?"

Rosa turned away looking pained, as if I'd just spoken of the dead. "You'll have to ask him about it. He's doing very well with the new restaurant in Alba, though. He aims to earn it a Michelin star, and will probably succeed."

As we drove away from the city and toward the countryside, I took in the scenery. Italy was like a prehistoric Vermont—lots of earthy colors and buildings that seemed to have sprouted from roots rather than been built. The sky was spectacular. The air smelled like pesto.

When we arrived at the Caramelli villa, an old-style, lemon-hued stucco façade with terra-cotta roof tiles, Luciana greeted us at the door and embraced me as if we were old friends. Near-identical features to her fraternal twin brother, only more curvy and longer hair. Luciana invited me in and led me straight to the kitchen—also decked in terra-cotta tile and organic colors of asparagus and turnips and blueberries, with framed family photos on the wall. In comparison to my stainless steel appliances, mosaic tiled backsplash and granite-countered kitchen, which I had always considered elegant albeit unoccupied, this one was downright *warm*, and not in the context of climate and temperature. If a room could hug you upon entering, this one would.

A cutting board loaded with breads, cheeses, and grapes took up a quarter of the table. And the table could sit eight. Two bottles of wine waited on call nearby.

Luciana gestured to the cheese display. "Please, help your-self. You must be famished."

I was, and my mouth salivated at the very sight, but how could I trust myself without my scale? Not to mention that, with the exception of the grapes, this was Code Orange. Lots and lots of Code Orange. Little devils as far as the eye could see.

"Thank you," I said, "but no. I'm okay."

As if she didn't hear me, Luciana picked up a white plate, filled it with one of everything, and handed it to me, followed by a stemmed glass of crisp Bianco. Unable to contain my lust—that's right, *lust*—for the sight of the bread, I broke a piece off and bit into it.

Oh my.

I was going to have to get out of this kitchen—and Genoa—and Italy—fast.

"So, we can leave for Alba first thing tomorrow and stay there for a day or two. It's about ninety minutes by car. Al-though I'm not sure where Luca is staying."

"In that case, I won't even bother to unpack."

"You'll get to see some of *la bella Italia*," said Rosa with a smile.

"In the meantime," said Luciana, "please eat. And rest. I'll even let you sleep in tomorrow, if you want."

"Thank you," I said, and devoured the rest of my cheese plate while we talked and became even more acquainted. Luciana refilled it, along with my glass of wine, and afterward she and Rosa showed me to my room complete with a balcony overlooking the pool and fountains in the backyard—*Hello, gorgeous. Wish you were here, Max*—and a bed that smelled like lavender and vanilla. And I'm talking the real deal, not some Glade plug-in air freshener. Rosa and Luciana spoke to each other in English rather than Italian, which, I thought, was quite courteous. I didn't speak a word of Italian (well, I knew a couple of words, *gelato* being one of them), and had downloaded an app on my phone the previous week to assist me. I'd been practicing ever since.

This would have made a good honeymoon location for Max and me. We'd opted for sun and sand, however, and chose a Sandals resort in Bermuda.

Tomorrow would have been our wedding day.

Despite the villa's remote, countryside appeal, as if removed not only from civilization but also the twenty-first century, it came equipped with all the modern-day amenities. I went to work handling emails, returning phone calls, and updating my calendar. I also searched Alba on Google Maps and Wikipedia—the only thing the city seemed to have going for it was its wine and truffle production. I imagined it as being rustic, with outdoor plumbing and sheep grazing in the streets. I hoped I was wrong.

five

Day One in Alba

"Sleeping in" wound up being me waking up at 7 a.m. (which would be 1 a.m. the previous night, New York time). It felt strange not to do my 5 a.m. workout. I wondered if a treadmill lived somewhere in this house, and if it would be rude for me to ask. What felt even stranger, however, was knowing that had I not found Max and Cheetah and the tangled sheets, I would have been spending this morning (or yesterday?) in a mad frenzy of changing into my wedding dress, having my hair and makeup done, and awaiting the delivery of flowers and photographers and the minister and coordinating with bridesmaids, all of whom were Max's friends. My younger sister was Maid of Honor; and yet, we'd barely done any of those typical bride/Maid of Honor things like mani-pedis and shopping for bridesmaid and groomsmen thank-you gifts and dog-earing countless pages in bridal magazines; my job simply demanded too much of me and I delegated all that stuff to assistants and wedding planners.

I would have skipped down the aisle blindly, obliviously, foolishly.

Would he have stopped it had I not caught him and Cheetah? Would he have ended the affair? Would he have prevented the wedding from happening? Would he have at least had enough respect to spare me the humiliation?

I showered and went downstairs to the kitchen to find breakfast waiting for me: freshly baked rolls with butter and jam. Biscotti, berries, and what looked to be some kind of latte in a round, ceramic cup the size of a Panera Bread soup bowl.

More bread.

We left for Alba around noon. Rosa made arrangements for the three of us to stay at an inn. Without intending to, I fell asleep in the car ten minutes into the trip, and was so crashed out that Rosa had to shake me awake, informing me that we had arrived.

"*Already?*" I asked.

"Took us two hours," said Rosa. We had to stop at the railroad crossing and wait for the train to pass."

"Let's go," said Luciana with a tone mixed with urgency and resolve. "We need surprise on our side."

"You didn't tell him we're coming?" I asked. "What if he's not there?"

"Oh, he'll be there," said Luciana. "If I know anything about my brother, it's that he lives for two things: pasta, and a challenge. He's got both with this restaurant."

We checked in and I used the bathroom before we got back in the car. Thankfully I was wrong about the outdoor plumbing. My reflection revealed a face seemingly belonging to someone other than a successful CEO: matted hair in need of a roots touch-up. Raccoon eyes, usually bright blue, but now tired turquoise. Frown lines on top of frown lines. Jet lag in 3-D. I combed my hair with my fingers and reapplied lipstick.

Where was Max right now? What did *he* look like? Was he aware of the date? Or was he off gallivanting with Cheetah, not giving me even a second of airtime in his head?

The driver zigzagged through the city streets (thankfully I was wrong about the sheep too) for about fifteen minutes until we hit a sparse part of town and a small house with a sign out front reading *Trattoria Naturale*.

For the first time, Luciana said something to Rosa in Italian in my presence. Her tone led me to deduce that whatever she said was condescending; however, I couldn't be sure at whom it was aimed—me, or her brother.

We entered a dining area that was about the size of my living room, filled to capacity with long, vertical tables in communal-style seating, and adorned with fresh flowers and bread baskets and bottles of wine. The aromas coming from the kitchen were positively fantasmic—I don't recall ever smelling something that actually made me feel like I was sitting in front of a fireplace on Christmas Eve, especially given that it was springtime. And yet, it felt . . . *weird*. The diners looked freakishly content. Like none of them had ever experienced a day of anguish in their lives. There also wasn't a smartphone in sight. People were actually talking—no, *conversing*. Listening. Laughing. And they were paying attention not only to one another but also to their food, every bite a conscious, deliberate act. Neither the mammoth, Olive Garden, one-serving-can-feed-a-family-of-four size portions nor the weighted-within-an-inch-of-its-life Pasta Pronto portions. These portions looked . . . *satisfying*.

I had never thought of Pasta Pronto's meals as unsatisfying. But I had also never thought of eating them as an exercise in mindfulness. If anything, I'd made it so that the consumer wouldn't have to think—or, more to the point, to *worry*. The calories were counted, the portion was measured, the taste was determined, and the meal was prepared. The purpose, of course, was to enjoy the pasta and not worry about the consequences. But the only consequence here seemed to be the enjoyment of the food itself, and the experience of eating it.

What if I had missed the point all along?

Without waiting for service, Luciana called out "Luca!" followed by what sounded like a command in Italian to get his ass out of the kitchen. Despite my wanting to shrink into my skin with embarrassment, the patrons didn't even look in her direction. I was surprised she didn't just barge into the kitchen. The kitchen door swung open and Gianluca Caramelli emerged in a chef's jacket and a bandana pushing back his hair.

There is such a thing as an Italian god. He's standing right in front of me. Tall. Statuesque. Formidable. *Perfecto.* The Instagram photos were downright ugly compared to the life-sized, three-dimensional, living, breathing Gianluca Caramelli.

He audibly responded when he saw his sister—and, subsequently, me beside her—by going into an Italian tirade, hand gestures and all.

"Luca, this is Katie Cravens," said Luciana calmly. "Katie, this is my twin brother, Gianluca." She followed up with something in Italian directed at him that I was sure translated as "Be nice."

I extended my hand and wore my biggest PR smile. "I'm very pleased to meet you," I said in Italian (I'd practiced last night). He looked at me with disgust, making me wonder if I'd accidentally said something else, like, "Your mother eats pig knuckles," and refused to shake my hand. Instead he turned to Luciana.

"What are you doing here? What is *she* doing here?" he asked. At least he spoke in English.

"*Katie* is here on business," said Luciana. "We can't move forward on the deal without your signature."

I chimed in a little more diplomatically, "I'm looking forward to working with you on an arrangement that is agreeable to everyone."

He went into a second tirade. "I'd just as soon eat scraps from the floor than put my name on anything that pretends to be food."

Luciana rolled her eyes around. "There you go again, Mister Drama."

He turned to me and bore a hole into my forehead with his fiery stare. "I'll bet you don't even know how to cut an onion."

I opened my mouth, waiting for sound to come out as if my voice were on a one-second delay. ". . . Like that proves anything about me. You foodie snobs are all alike. Just because someone comes up with something that's quick and easy and tastes good and people like it, you're ready to crucify them. So I manufacture frozen food. So I eat spaghetti from a box. Big deal. Like you've never bought anything from Starbucks or that came in a can or something."

He laughed. Out loud. Like, it echoed in the ceiling beams. And it sounded like pots and pans banging together.

I pressed my lips together, tightly, feeling my face turn hot with humiliation. I should have slapped him. Should have told him where he could put his pasta and stormed out, screw the deal. But no, I wasn't going to give Gianluca Caramelli the satisfaction of making me feel like a piece of discarded gum stuck to the bottom of a shoe.

Luciana scolded him in Italian. He defiantly crossed his arms before giving in and offering me a brusque apology.

I huffed in acknowledgment. "Don't do me any favors," I said. And still, no one around us seemed to be paying attention to anything but one another and their meals.

Gianluca looked me up and down, not in an overt sexual way but almost clinical, diagnostic, even. Could probably see right through my clothes, like Superman. Then he took my hand, led me to a table, and seated me. "First, you eat. Then we speak business."

Minutes later he returned with tomato and arugula on crostini with fresh mozzarella, and poured a glass of wine from one of the bottles on the table.

"In Italy, lunch is the biggest meal of the day. This is the *antipasto* course. The arugula and tomatoes came from the garden out back. The mozzarella was made from goat's milk. The bread was made this morning from locally farmed wheat and chicken eggs."

"Hang on," I said. "I can't eat more than one course."

"I'm not doing any business with you unless you eat every course I serve you. No one who claims to be passionate about food should be as skinny as you are. It's unnatural."

In all my life, no one ever called me skinny as an insult.

"Being passionate about food doesn't mean you have to eat *all* of it," I said. "So I want to be able to keep on wearing strapless dresses. Sue me."

He turned to Luciana, saying, "And you think *I'm* dramatic?" before returning his attention to me, shaking his head in exasperation. "You Americans and your distorted body image. I think the cola companies put a secret chemical in all those diet soft drinks that make you see yourselves the wrong way."

His accent was divine, even when he was being rude.

Gianluca pushed the plate closer to me. "I can sit here all day," he said. "Eat."

"So can I," I retorted. "You can't force me to eat. Especially not as blackmail. And quite frankly, I don't see how my eating habits are any of your business. Literally."

He raised his hands in surrender. A little too quickly, if you ask me. "Whatever you say. But you're missing out on the best food in Italy."

He began to pull the plate away, but my hand reflexively grabbed it. "I didn't say to take it away. I just said I didn't want to eat a ten-course meal or whatever."

Gianluca smiled. A full-toothed, glistening white, dissolve-in-a-puddle-of-your-own-drool smile.

I peered at his left hand, still holding the plate. *No ring*.

"Tell you what, Miss Katie," said Gianluca. "I'll sign the contracts, but with one stipulation."

I braced myself. *I am* not *sleeping with you; I don't care how hot you are.*

Then again . . .

"And what is that? I have to lick the plate clean after I eat everything on it? Scrub the pots?"

Luca shook his head again, enjoying his little manipulation games. "No," he said. "First you have to learn how to cook. And eat. And live. And I'm going to show you how."

six

"You've got some nerve," I said in response to Gianluca's smarmy little proposal. "What do you know about me? Nothing. What makes you think I need to learn how to cook? Just because I didn't go to some famous cooking school?"

"I didn't go to cooking school either," said Gianluca. "Unless you count my grandfather Vincenzo's kitchen."

The way he spoke his grandfather's name—*Vincenzo*—so much love and passion.

"You know what I mean. Just because I don't *like* to cook doesn't mean I don't know *how* to."

Truth was, at one time I did like to cook. When I was a teenager, I'd opted for *Woman's Day* over *Seventeen* magazines so I could cut out and file recipes. I made my first meatloaf in the ninth grade, and my first roasted chicken for high school graduation, although I forgot to check the time and burned it to a crisp. My mashed potatoes were legendary, although I'm not sure in a good way.

So what changed? College, for one. Cooking took a back-seat to studying and socializing. Ramen noodles replaced roasted chicken. Sandwiches replaced salads. Meal plans and the Freshman Twenty, formerly the Freshman Fifteen, when you gained twenty pounds in your first year of college mostly as the result of all-you-can-eat cereal in the dining hall. Always a flabby kid, not to mention an overachiever, I progressed to sophomore year not only with a 3.8 GPA but also ten pounds over the Freshman Twenty. If Butterball needed a human representation, I was first in line for the position.

Not to mention my mother giving me the once-over when I came home for Christmas and reproving me with, *"You look just like your father."*

In the summer following sophomore year, I dieted down to ten pounds under my entering freshman weight. Yet cooking still didn't make the cut. Instead I ate salads galore and watched my portions like a hawk and cut out all carbs and ran the track every morning. I tried just about every frozen food diet entrée on the market and came up dissatisfied. But I was determined to beat the deprivation of my beloved pasta. The only way to do that was to start my own product line and company. So eventually I did, and that sealed my fate when it came to cooking versus convenience.

In the present moment, Gianluca laughed again, loud and boisterous. If anyone from the States laughed like that, I'd have assumed they were exaggerating, even faking it. But I could tell Gianluca's laugh was the real deal, and it only infuriated me more. Which, I suspected, was exactly what he wanted to do.

As if I weren't standing there, Gianluca turned to his twin sister and said, "Look who you're getting into business with. Someone who doesn't like to cook."

"*We* are getting into business with someone who has excellent credentials and is as passionate about her work as you are about yours," said Luciana. "Plus she knows how to run a company, which is more than I can say for you, *gemella mia*."

For the first time, Gianluca looked like he'd been unnerved, even wounded. As if he and his sister were little kids and she'd just teased him.

Without saying another word, he stormed back into the kitchen. I looked at Rosa and Luciana, who both looked unfazed. "Is he coming back out?" I asked.

"He's getting your next course," said Luciana.

I raised a hand and shook my head in refusal, but passing on food from this family was futile. Moments later Gianluca returned with a plate of trofie pasta with basil pesto sauce and set it in front of me. "I made the trofie myself," he said. "The pesto is made with fresh basil from the garden, and drizzled with extra virgin olive oil and a drop of lemon juice. *Buon appetito*."

He held out a clean fork. I shot him a glare and was met with a smug smile as I took it. All three of them watched and waited for me to take a bite. I speared one of the trofie and first brought it to my nose for a whiff. From the corner of my eye, I saw Gianluca smile in satisfaction, as if I'd finally done something right. Then I brought the fork to my mouth, inserted it, and closed my eyes as the flavors touched my taste buds, one by one.

The trofie: perfectly al dente and practically melting in my mouth. The basil: pungent, but not overpowering. The lemon: such a little touch of flavor brought the entire dish to a whole new level of taste.

Oh. My God. Yes.

Yes!

YES!!!

And then it slipped out. A cross between an *mmmmmmm* and an *ohhhhhhhhhh*.

"*That* is what pasta tastes like," said Gianluca. "I'll bet your plastic abominations never tasted like that."

And just like that, he ruined my food orgasm. And how does an Italian know the word *abomination*? I mean, his English was as flawless as his sister's, but still.

I let the fork clatter on the plate and pushed it away in defiance. Forget how fantasmic it tasted. "Look, *Mister* . . ."

"Luca," he said, smiling in a taunting way. The ends of his hair were damp from sweat, making him look even sexier.

"Nobody likes when you spike the football after you score the touchdown. A simple thank-you would have sufficed. And I have no intention of being coerced into going into business with anyone. You don't want to do the deal, fine. Your loss. I don't need to learn how to cook. Or eat. Or live. My life isn't some Elizabeth Gilbert book. I'm doing very well, thank you."

A soft, yet audible burp escaped from me.

Rosa leaned over and whispered, "You're in what you would call soccer country. No one here knows American football."

Shit-fritters.

Luca held up his hands as if to say, *Oh well*. "It was nice to meet you," he said. "*Ciao*." And with that he picked up the plates and carried them back to the kitchen. This time Luciana followed him in, and I could hear them arguing in Italian for the next five minutes.

I looked at Rosa, mortified on behalf of the entire restaurant clientele. "You know, in the States, people would give a restaurant an unfavorable review for such behavior among the establishment's owners."

"This is a different kind of restaurant," she replied. "It's not meant to be so formal like an American place. It's like being together with your family."

My thoughts went to Olive Garden. Yeah, so not what they had in mind when they came up with *that* slogan.

My intention had been to come here and personally persuade Gianluca that our culinary collaboration would be a good match, but suddenly I had my doubts. Had Pasta Pronto and the Caramellis' restaurant not been in financial trouble, would we ever have crossed paths, even dreamed of going into business together? This was a marriage of convenience, not true love. Which then got me thinking about Max. What had attracted me to him? Was it those finely tailored suits he wore to court every day? Was it the way he could tie a knot with a cherry stem in his mouth? Was it that he was home from work precisely at 7 p.m. every night, always took out the garbage and left the toilet seats down without being asked, selected the perfect Christmas gifts for me by asking my personal assistant to make a list? Was it that he was good (albeit predictable) in bed?

Maybe that's what I loved about Max. He was reliable. Until he came home with coconut shrimp and a woman in *my* bed. *Our* bed.

But I had thought Max was true love. True love could also be dependable and reliable, couldn't it?

I wasn't sure of anything anymore, except that I was going to make *this* work. My company needed it to.

Luca and Luciana reemerged from the kitchen.

"Gianluca, you want to teach me how to cook? Fine. You want to belittle me and laugh in my face? Be my guest. But I am not leaving here until you sign those contracts. And when you do, Pasta Pronto and the Caramellis will go together like mac and cheese," I said.

Okay, so maybe I should have left off the mac and cheese part.

Gianluca—*Luca*—furrowed his brow, as if we were a life-size game of chess and I'd just put him in check. It only took him seconds, however, to figure out my strategy, and his frown morphed into a sly grin as he answered with his own. "Okay. You do that."

Wait, what?

He one-upped my dare. "I like to know whom I'm getting involved with, as you say in the States. You can stay here in Alba."

Luciana pulled me aside. "This is an excellent plan, Katie. Luca needs to be able to trust you. Spend a few days here, watch him work, and let him show you how to make a couple of dishes. Humor him. And while you're here, get a peek at the books if you can. I think he could really use your expertise and organization."

But . . .

I looked at Rosa chatting with Luca, and then made eye contact with him. He acknowledged me and smiled. "Is it a deal, Miss Katie?"

seven

Day Two in Alba

So this was where my stubbornness got me: a little city in Italy, with a hot guy who hated me (and I wasn't too keen on him either), trying to convince him to join forces and make marketable pasta meals by kowtowing to his every move.

I suppose it could have been worse. He could have been a pastry chef.

Not to mention it completely derailed all preoccupied thoughts about my would-have-been wedding day. This was a good thing.

I woke up at the inn the next morning around 8 a.m., still feeling the effects of jet lag. Also, what was this, day three of no workout? My joints squeaked and popped as I stretched. Perhaps I could do a couple of crunches before Luca met me in the parlor. We had agreed to meet so that I could go "behind the scenes" in the kitchen of Trattoria Naturale, and Luca would presumably give me a cooking lesson as well.

My stomach rumbled as I strolled into the lobby at nine-thirty wearing jeans, ballerina flats, and a light, short-sleeved pink sweater with a low scoop-neck. The one that made me feel sexy and luxurious, I confess. Used to be Max's favorite. Luca, however, wearing blue jeans that he was practically born into, a finely knit black T-shirt, and nubuck hiking boots (the man looked like the Pinocchio of Prada, turned into a real boy after years of living in a *Vogue* magazine ad), seemed unimpressed with my sweater, or me. And this was after he ambled in a half-hour late.

"Good morning," I said before adding, "Did you forget to set your alarm clock or something?"

"I don't use an alarm clock," he replied before adding, "You're pale."

"Um, in case you're wondering, the proper English phrase for *buon giorno* is 'good morning,' not 'you're pale,'" I shot back.

"You don't eat enough," he said. "I can tell. You haven't eaten anything this morning. Why is that?"

"I usually skip breakfast—and don't tell me it's the most important meal of the day," I interjected before he could even open his mouth. "I'm convinced Bisquick or a cereal company came up with that idea so they could sell more product."

Luca rolled his eyes. Interesting that such an annoying gesture was universal.

"First of all, *every* meal is the most important of the day. Second, you're in Italy—your days of 'Bisquick' are over."

"You make it sound like I'm never going back to New York."

"Maybe you won't want to."

"*Yeah, right,*" I said as we walked to his Ferrari Testarossa. Red, of course. *I'll bet he calls her Lola.* "New York is the greatest place in the world, with some of the best restaurants in the world, including Caramelli's—when it was still open, that is." My attempt to suck up at the last minute collapsed like an overdone soufflé.

Luca chortled. "The New York Caramelli's was like those cartoon portraits that those city artists do on the streets for the tourists."

"Caricatures?"

"Yes, caricatures. We built brick walls and ovens and bought cast iron pots and pans and made the menu almost identical to Genoa's, but it wasn't *real*. It didn't have my grandfather's blood, sweat, and tears in it. You couldn't hear his voice. You couldn't feel his heartbeat. That's why all the other locations failed. They had no soul."

"I heard it's because people didn't think your food was so hot—I mean good, not temperature."

Luca glared at me, then opened the passenger door for me before walking around to his side. At least he had date etiquette, although the last thing I would call this was a date. "I know what 'hot' is in U.S. vernacular. I've lived in New York on and off since I was a teenager. I even considered applying for dual citizenship. I'll bet you didn't know that."

I didn't. Google fail.

"So then you know how great it is," I said.

He shrugged his shoulders. "It's great because somebody sold you its greatness. That's the thing with people like you, Miss Katie. You buy and sell everything. My mission in life has always been to *make* something."

I perused the dashboard for something to break.

"First of all, I *made* my company and my pasta line. I hired the best food technicians in the business. I learned the ins and outs of being a CEO and a manufacturer. I taste every single pasta dish before it hits the market. If I don't like it, we don't sell it. Second of all, *people like you*? Do you have any idea how insulting and closed-minded a phrase that is? To say nothing of the fact that you still don't know anything about me."

"Where do you live, exactly?" he asked.

"Dix Hills," I replied. "It's about an hour from the city by train on Long Island. But it's still New York. And Pasta Pronto's headquarters is in the city."

He shook his head and muttered something under his breath, as if I'd just proved his point.

"What?" I said. "Share your answers with the class."

"Have you ever lived *in* the city?"

"No," I said, unable to quash the sheepish feeling that was seeping in. "But so what?"

"You know nothing. You know nothing about New York. You've never bought fresh fruit from the farmers markets. You've never been inside the kitchen of a restaurant that wasn't owned by some celebrity or corporate chain and smelled the ingredients and tasted the sauces from a wooden spoon. You've never talked to the people or even looked them in the eye, probably."

"Who's selling something now? Everything you just described is just some lofty idea of living. Well, guess what? It's not *my* idea of living. So I like being in the suburbs with a swimming pool and a basement. So I eat meals that don't require hours of chopping and slicing and dicing and rot if you don't eat them twenty seconds after you make them. So I prefer convenience to cooking, given my busy schedule. That doesn't make me less of a person than you."

"Whatever you say, Miss Katie," he said, not taking his eyes off the road. "And let me tell you why people didn't like the menu—it was too Italian for them. Any American who says they love Italian food doesn't know what it is. They love spaghetti and meatballs and red sauce. That's all they want. They don't know what real, authentic Genoa food is. They don't know how many different varieties of pasta there are. They think it's good if you add cream to it."

"You're a pasta troll," I said. "That's what I'm going to call you from now on. Luca the Pasta Troll."

"I'm proud to accept that title."

"What's wrong with spaghetti and red sauce? I happen to be one of those Americans who love spaghetti and red sauce. It's what made me fall in love with pasta in the first place."

"Then why didn't you learn to make it for yourself rather than settling for a frozen fake?"

Good question. It never occurred to me to do so. I was more about staving off calories and carbs than adding to them.

The scenery suddenly became unfamiliar. "Where are we going?" I asked. "I don't remember this route to the restaurant."

"We're going to get you your breakfast. Always eat food in season. Berries are in season right now. We're going to pick some berries—"

"Excuse me, did you say *pick* some berries?"

"Well, from a bushel basket, this time. My excellent friend Enzo has already harvested them—"

"Because I am so not dressed for berry-picking."

Luca ignored me. "And then we're going to go to the trattoria and whip up some cream and make some scones, and that will be your breakfast. Where does that rate on your little rainbow chart?"

I shot him a look. "You know about Pasta Pronto's color coding system?"

"I do my homework too, Miss Katie."

I silently did the rankings: Berries: Fruit. Good. Code Green. Cream: Dairy. Bad. Orange. Scones: Carbs. *Molto male*. Red.

"Can I just have the berries and skip the scones and cream?"

He shook his head in exasperation again. "This is what I'm saying. You've got it all wrong. There's no such thing as a bad food if it's natural. Food is life. Say it with me: *food is life*."

I said nothing.

He continued to goad me. "Come on, Miss Katie, say it: food is life."

"This is silly."

Luca slammed on the brakes and put the car in park in the middle of the road.

"Are you crazy???" I yelled. Cars behind him honked and swerved around us.

"Say it," he said.

"I'm not saying it."

A mischievous grin appeared as he tapped his fingers on the steering wheel. "We'll stay here all day long."

"How 'bout I say this instead: you're an asshole. How do you say *that* in Italian?"

"*Sei un stronzo*," he practically sang before laughing gleefully, and my thighs tingled. "Say it, Miss Katie. Say it, say it, say it!"

"*Sei un stronzo!*" I yelled, and he let out another explosion of laughter.

"The other thing," he forced out between giggle fits. "Say the other thing."

"*FOOD IS LIFE*, okay? Now will you move this car, you immature Italian foodie freakboy?"

And with that he stopped laughing, put the car in gear, and drove on.

We went to Luca's friend Enzo's strawberry farm (or was it a patch? Or an orchard?), where he and Luca talked for a good fifteen minutes in Italian (he didn't share his twin sister's manners in that particular aspect) before introducing me. Unlike Luca, Enzo was more burly and less sculpted. He was way friendlier, however, and made an attempt to speak to me in broken English, offering me fresh strawberries and showing me his herb garden. After that, we drove to Trattoria Naturale—it was just getting ready to open at noon—and Luca escorted me to the kitchen. The setup was small and simple, yet everything was within reach: stove, pantry, freezer, pots and pans and spoons and knives and ladles and cutting boards of all shapes and sizes, to say nothing of plates and flatware and wine glasses, and a door leading to what I presumed was a wine cellar. Although completely lacking any décor or windows, somehow I could feel a welcoming ambiance not unlike what I felt the moment I entered Luciana's kitchen in the villa.

Luca put on his chef's jacket and bandana (and what was it about that simple piece of clothing and accessory that made him even sexier? Was it a guys-in-uniform thing?), and placed the basket of strawberries on one of the cutting boards. In a whirl-wind he grabbed a bottle of cream, a bottle of what I guessed was buttermilk, judging by the color, a ginormous canister of flour, two other canisters, and several sticks of butter, and went to work on the scones after washing his hands, measuring each ingredient quickly but precisely, and all by memory.

"I thought you were going to teach me how to cook," I said, standing on the other side of the workstation, watching him in a dizzy frenzy as he added cubes of butter and mixed the dough with his hands.

"Oh, so now you want to learn?" he asked, not looking up from the bowl.

"I didn't say that. I just figured you'd tell me the recipe as you went along, or were going to somehow get me involved."

"I'll do that when we make the pasta. For now, just watch."

Luca scooped a handful of flour from the canister and sprinkled it on the cutting board before spreading it around with his fingers. He then transferred the dough from the bowl to the board, divided the dough in half, and grabbed a rolling pin. He was about to continue when he stopped and reconsidered. "Do you want to roll out the dough?"

"Me?"

Duh!

"Okay." I washed my hands and joined him next to the cutting board. He smelled like strawberries and vanilla and a spice I couldn't identify. I'd never smelled such scents on a guy before, but vanilla plus man essence? *Wow.*

The rolling pin wasn't the kind with the handle grips. I tentatively took hold of the corners. Luca moved and stood behind me, lording several inches over me in height, and re-positioned my hands with his own. "Don't hold it like corn on the cob. *Grasp* it," he said. His hands felt rough to the touch. He scooped another handful of flour and stroked the rolling pin with it, a powdery cloud blowing into my face and on my sweater. Then, clasping my wrists, he brought the pin to the dough. "Don't be afraid of it," he said of the dough. "You're not going to break it. Just don't roll it out too much."

"I'm not *afraid* of it," I countered. "You're just crushing my wrists, is all."

And the scent of you is making me want to roll you in this flour.

His grip loosened. Together we finished rolling out the dough, and he cut about a dozen wedges and laid them on two greased baking sheets, melted some butter and brushed it on the wedges, and placed the sheets in the oven without using protective mitts.

"Now what?" I asked.

He pushed the empty bowl and rolling pin aside and wiped down the cutting board with a damp towel. Then he collected a clean mixing bowl, a canister of powdered sugar, the bottle of cream, and a whisk. "Now we whip the cream," he said.

Luca poured the cream into the bowl without measuring, and added a spoonful of the powdered sugar. "We don't need much of this," he said of the sugar. "Just enough to sweeten it a little."

"How do you know how much goes in without measuring it?" I asked.

"After a while you get to know just by looking at it." He extended the whisk to me. "Want to do the whipping?"

Man, was *that* a loaded question.

"You don't need an electric mixer?"

"My grandfather never did," he replied.

I took the whisk and dropped it into the bowl, turning it in a circular motion. Luca impatiently grabbed the whisk out of my hands as he pushed me aside with his body.

"Ouch!" I said. "You suck at the whole hands-on approach."

"You don't *stir* with a whisk! You . . . you *whisk* it. You beat the cream into submission."

I watched as the whisk—now an extension of his arm and hand—rotated with the same velocity as a beater on an electric mixer set to High. As if Luca had superpowers. Within minutes the cream transformed from liquid to solid, forming soft peaks in the bowl. He dabbed the whipped cream from the tip of the whisk onto his fingertip, and inserted it between his lips. "*Perfecto!*" he said. "Here . . ." He gestured for me to hold out my hand, and he dabbed my finger with the tip of the cream-covered whisk as well. "Taste."

I brought my finger to my mouth and licked. Luca didn't take his eyes off me.

Oh my. And I thought Cool Whip was heaven in a plastic tub.

"That is a-ma-zing," I said.

"Wait until you taste with the strawberries and scones. You will want to name your first child after me. As you should."

I frowned. "Why do you do that?" I said.

"Do what?"

"Ruin every tasting by being a self-centered jerk. Why can't you just say 'thank you' like any other nice, normal human being? Seriously, it kills the pleasure, not to mention the aftertaste. You might as well have added arsenic to the whipped cream."

For the first time since we'd met, Luca looked genuinely remorseful. His dark eyes turned away, sad and sorry. Without so much as a glance in my direction or saying another word, he hulled and sliced a dozen strawberries in record speed. By the time he finished, the scones were ready. He set them on a rack to cool, relocated the whipped cream to the refrigerator, and trotted out to the dining area where the tables were being set. Not knowing what else to do, I followed him back and forth like a stray puppy. He still didn't say a word, to me, the workers cleaning windows and tables and chairs and sweeping floors, or the cooks prepping in the kitchen. It was as if Gianluca Caramelli was invisible, nothing more than a gust of wind swirling around.

Luca motioned me to the table I'd sat at the previous day. As I approached, he held the chair and politely seated me, finally with a gentle touch. Apparently his manners ebbed and flowed. He disappeared into the kitchen. Five minutes later, he returned with a tray of photoshoot-ready plated scones, strawberries, and whipped cream, their red and white and gold hues sparkling like sunlight on the stark white plates.

He sliced a scone and topped it with the cream and strawberries, each one delicately placed rather than dropped or dolloped, and served it to me.

"Eat with your hands," he said as an invitation rather than a command. They were the first words he'd spoken in at least ten minutes, if not longer. He served himself, yet didn't take a bite until he watched me take one first.

The flavors—my God, the *flavors*! If there was such a thing as food soul mates, then these strawberries and scones and cream were eternally bonded.

This was what springtime tasted like.

"I have no words," I said with my mouth full.

Luca smiled. "Thank you," he said, his voice soft and amiable. Two bites later and he added, "Our first meal, Miss Katie. Now that wasn't so bad, was it?"

eight

After our brunch of strawberries and scones and a cup of espresso that made Red Bull seem like a sleep aid, I asked Luca if I could work in the restaurant office while he continued with his chef responsibilities.

"Sure," he said. "I don't think Alberto will mind."

"Alberto?" I asked.

"The owner."

"I thought *you* were the owner."

"I'm kind of like a not-so-silent partner. I'm putting in my expertise and name, but Alberto put in most of the capital."

"Alberto is also a chef, yes?"

"*Sì*. Yes."

"So, you're not drawing a salary?"

"I'm not in this business for the money," he said.

"I see. So your Gucci shoes and that car out there is slumming it?"

Luca frowned. "You said you had work to do, Miss Katie?" He pointed to a door. "There's the office."

I returned his glare. "Thank you," I said, and I entered and closed the door behind me. It was about 6 p.m. in New York, thus not an ideal time for making phone calls to Pasta Pronto HQ or Jennifer, my personal assistant. Instead I tackled my email inbox, reducing the deluge to a mere trickle. Being a CEO was a never-ending job of decision-making and problem-solving, and each email detailed a fire that needed putting out, a deadline that must be met, a matter demanding immediate attention, and so on. Well, *every* matter demanded immediate attention; the trick was triaging the order of urgency, like in an Emergency Room. Next, I checked Pasta Pronto's stock value against rival companies and reviewed the agenda for the upcoming board meeting. For the first time in I couldn't remember how long, I faced an empty schedule for the remainder of the week. No reminders from Siri. No appointments with the acupuncturist or the accountant or the executive team. No meetings or press releases or conference calls or visits to the factory.

Truth be told, it kind of frightened me. What was I supposed to do with all that time?

Two hours later, I stopped for a break and took in my surroundings—not much to look at, really. A snug space. A bulletin board with post-it notes in Italian scrawl. A calendar on the wall, with this month's photo depicting a beach sunset with palm trees; seemed like a very American thing. The desk was uncluttered, but succumbing to the temptation of nosiness, I opened the front drawer and found it littered with receipts, invoices, contracts, check stubs, you name it. I actually gasped at the disarray, albeit quietly. As my hands swam through the paper swamp, I felt compelled to sort through and organize them, but couldn't make sense of them due to the language.

The door opened and I nearly jumped out of the chair—how did I not hear the footsteps?

"Ahhh, you've found our dirty little secret," said a man who could pass for George Clooney's younger brother.

Busted.

"I . . . I was looking for a pen," I stammered, and could feel my face flushing, no doubt the color of the strawberries I'd consumed earlier, when I spotted a blue ballpoint resting comfortably and conspicuously next to my iPad.

"It's okay," he said with a welcoming smile rather than accusatory glower. "There's no need for you to be . . ." He seemed not to know the word.

I offered a few: "Embarrassed? Ashamed? Mortified?"

He chuckled and sat in the chair beside the desk.

"You must be Alberto," I said. "My name is Katie Cravens. I'm . . ." What was I doing here, exactly? Oh, right. Saving my company.

He shook my hand.

"It's a pleasure to meet you, *Signorina* Cravens." He pointed to the deluge of papers in the drawer. "I think I might have gotten myself into trouble when I joined our dear friend Luca in this business," he said.

He's not my *friend*, I wanted to say, but I stayed on topic. "How so?"

"Luca . . . he has no patience for this," he said, gesturing to the open drawer. "He spends money without caring how it balances out on the other side. It's all in service of the food. But he forgets that the food is only one part of survival."

"He's rather spoiled," I offered.

Alberto shook his head in deference. "His family provided him with everything he needed, yes, and he never wanted for anything. But when Vincenzo died, God rest his soul"—Alberto gestured the sign of the cross, beginning at his forehead and ending at his heart—"I think he took Luca's heart with him. They were very, very close."

I tried to imagine Gianluca as a boy—innocent, idealistic, piercing eyes round and full of hope and wonder, his hair tousled and cowlicked, at his grandfather's side in a rustic kitchen. I'd seen photos of Vincenzo Caramelli when I'd researched the family, and again at the Caramelli villa: old-worldly, with leathery skin and thinning gray hair—as if he'd been born with it—slicked back and a faint mustache. Dressed in simple shirt and trousers made by Maria Caramelli, his wife of forty-plus years. A man of few words, but powerful in presence. A robust smile and demeanor.

"He was sixty when he died unexpectedly of a heart attack, devastating a fifteen-year-old Luca and the restaurant world," said Luciana.

"I'm sorry," I said. "I don't really know Luca. In fact, I didn't meet him until yesterday."

"He's a good man. He just needs to learn how to live a little. He needs to learn how to love again. He pours all his love into his food, but saves nothing for the people he serves it to."

Gianluca Caramelli needs to learn how to live? I thought that was what he was supposed to teach me. As for the love, well, it seemed that I could use lessons myself. After all, had I been better at it, I would have been on my honeymoon in Bermuda right now rather than stuck in Alba trying to save my company with a whisk.

Alberto tacked on, "And I need help with all of this," he said of the papers.

"I'm surprised you don't have all of this on computer," I said.

"Luca likes to do things the way his grandfather did. I have no head for business or computers. I told Luca that. He said, 'Leave it to me.' I shouldn't have taken his word for it."

"Perhaps I could help you," I heard myself say. What on earth had possessed me to say it? Like I knew anything about running a restaurant. Other than waiting tables at a TGI Fridays in college one semester, I had no experience whatsoever.

"But perhaps you shouldn't tell Luca," I added. "I don't think he likes me very much."

"A beautiful girl like you?" he said, and I couldn't help but smile coyly. It had been quite some time since a man said anything flattering—or genuine—to me. Any kind word Max had ever uttered to me was now called into question, attached with an asterisk. Alberto quickly scanned the rest of me, not unlike the way Luca did the previous day. "Of course, you could use a bit more flesh," he said, pointing to my hips before excusing himself and leaving the office.

Now there's a first.

Rather than take the traditional nap following lunch, I worked all through siesta. Luca was busy tending to the garden behind the restaurant, and later he was in the kitchen. If I didn't know any better, I would have thought he was avoiding me. Alberto permitted me to empty the drawer of paperwork into my briefcase and take it back to the inn with me; I figured I could call Luciana and/or Rosa and ask them to help me translate and decipher it all.

Luca took me back to the inn around six o'clock. Despite doing so little in terms of physical and mental exertion, I felt as if I'd put in a fourteen-hour day at HQ. Was I still jet-lagged? Or was I so burnt out that the exhaustion was working its way out of my system like the flu?

"So what do you think, Miss Katie?" asked Luca.

"About what?" I asked.

"About the things you saw today."

I saw Luca in his natural habitat. I saw bushels of strawberries. I saw people eating with pleasure.

I shrugged my shoulders. "I'm not sure what I'm supposed to think."

"It's a simple life, yes?"

"Running a restaurant is simple?" I asked, thinking about the drawer stuffed with papers in the office. "Doesn't seem so."

"Beats running a corporation in New York."

"Perhaps. If simple is what you want."

"You don't like simplicity?" he asked.

"I don't like *boredom*," I said. "Granted, I don't like being scheduled up to my eyeballs either, but I do like having a job where no day is repeated and I have plenty of interaction. I like to be productive. I don't like to sit still."

"Did you see me sitting still today?"

"No. But a farm-to-table nook in Alba is light-years away from a full-scale restaurant in Manhattan. Or being the CEO of a Fortune 500 corporation."

"You can be a CEO or a Manhattan chef and still live a simple life," he offered.

"I don't see how," I replied. "And it sounds to me like you're sold on the idea of simplicity rather than living it for yourself."

"Hardly," he said with a huff. After a pause, he asked, "Do you live life on your own terms, Miss Katie?"

"What? Of course I do!"

He shook his head slightly in skepticism. "I left the family business because it stopped being something I believed in. That's why I'm so against your merger. I don't believe in what you sell. I don't believe in your way of thinking. I have to live life the way I want, not the way my twin sister or my parents or anyone else thinks it should be."

"So then why am I even here if you're so dead set against it?" I asked.

"I love a challenge."

Was that a dare? A threat? Was he hitting on me?

"So do I," I said.

"I can see that. You wouldn't be here if you didn't. So let's challenge each other and see who wins."

"I'm not here to play games, Luca."

He pulled the car up to the inn, put it in park, and turned to me. "Aren't you?" His dark eyes suddenly glowed like cats' eyes, and shot sparks right into mine, which traveled straight south.

I opened the car door, stepped out, and leaned in before I slammed it. "Luca, not only am I not here to play games, but I'm also not here to learn simplicity, or pick strawberries, or whatever you think I'm sorely lacking in my existence. I live life on *my* own terms too. If an employee doesn't produce, I fire them. If sales go down, I get them back up. If my fiancé cheats on me, I kick him out. I'm not your plaything, and I'm not your challenge. Either get on board with this partnership and sign the damn contracts, or get out of my way."

And with that, I slammed the car door, turned my back on Luca, and walked toward the inn's entrance.

My stomach growled. I had forgotten to eat again. And I had four unscheduled hours before bedtime waiting for me.

nine

There are two kinds of people in this world: those who get over breakups quickly and easily, and normal people. The former people are called *liars*.

Since Max and I broke up, not a day passed where I didn't go to sleep or wake up missing the way he draped his arm across my back or let his leg cross the bed and intermingle with mine. Not a day passed where I didn't long to re-familiarize myself with the tickle of his beard against my cheek, or the scent of him the moment he exited the shower, a combination of soap and steam (yes, steam has a smell) and that one-of-a-kind eau-de-Max aroma that couldn't be bot-tled (which was probably a good thing because I'd have been hoarding cases of it). Not a day passed where I didn't hear the phantom ring of my name in the sound of his voice, taunting, beckoning, pleading, "Kaaaattieeeeee . . ."

Time heals all wounds, they say.

It'll get easier, they say.

They lie. It doesn't.

Because time has a way of messing with your memory and making you doubt the truth. And it's those things you *don't* miss that screw with you more than those you do. For example: dirty socks on the floor. Every single night, Max left his dirty socks on the floor. They convened in a pile like a band of happy vagrants around a campfire. Worse yet was when he rummaged through them, selected one, and smelled it to see if it would pass muster for clean after opening his top dresser drawer and finding it sockless. Max and I had a rule: he did his laundry and I did mine. The only time our underwear was permitted to fraternize was when it was on (and soon to come off) our bodies. And he obliged just fine, except he always forgot to add his socks to the washing machine. Thus, Max's dirty sock solution was never to wash them—no, it was buy more socks. By our tenth anniversary, I would have been wading knee-deep in a sea of dirty socks.

How did I ever think this would be okay with me? How did I never think it through? It's not like I thought his behavior would change. I just plain never thought about it at all, other than to constantly complain about it.

And then there was the whole fart thing. He *cheered* for them. Cheered for his farts! The man went to Harvard! He passed the bar exam on the first shot! He'd been published in *Harvard Law Review*! Yet there he was, pumping his fist in the air after cutting one and giving it a score and saying things like "well done." I was mortified whenever it happened to me, even in private. Made me mortified when it happened to him too. If the cheering thing was supposed to downplay the embarrassment, well, it had the opposite effect on me.

And while we're on the subject: farts are proof of a vengeful God. Even the word stinks.

How did I fall in love with such a man? That's what I found myself asking as presently I lay in bed alone, in the dark, hungry. If I could be so blind to such irksome qualities, then it's no surprise that I missed the whopping one of his cheating on me. His solution wasn't to clean the socks, but buy new ones. He did the same with relationships. When we first dated, he told me he'd "grown tired" of his last girlfriend, that she didn't excite him the way I did, didn't challenge him, didn't stimulate his intellect or his nether-regions. How did I not see the pattern? He just bought himself a new girlfriend. And when he tired of *me*, when he no longer found me "appetizing," he found someone whom he did.

Should I visit Cheetah at the Cheesecake Factory and warn her about him? Would she listen, or would she take it as the ranting of a crazy woman desperate to get her ex back? I knew I would.

Did I still *want* him back? And how could I ask that question of someone I was so ready to marry, about whom I was once so certain? Would I have awakened one day, years into the marriage, and come to the realization that *Oh my God, I was totally wrong about this guy*?

Of course, the more frightening thought was that Cheetah was *the one*. The one that would make him stop tossing dirty socks. The one who would stimulate and satisfy him for the rest of his life. Why couldn't *I* have been enough? I have an MBA. Aside from Oprah and Martha Stewart, I became the most successful female CEO before the age of thirty-five. I worked out and never let my roots show and didn't bite my nails and shaved every day and got my eyebrows waxed and made sure I was bikini-ready for all seasons.

What on earth was I lacking?

How could I trust my judgment about anything anymore? How could I make a sound decision about what, or whom, I wanted for my life? How could I know what was good for me? I couldn't even trust a scone. I had no problem making decisions about my company. Had no problem trusting my instincts there, and trusting that I surrounded myself with smart people who also trusted their instincts, and whose instincts were often right on the money, literally.

This was why I hated being in Alba without a schedule, I realized. Working twelve-to-fourteen-hour days and getting up for 5 a.m. workouts never gave me time to *think* about all this stuff. Now I had all the time in the world, and I couldn't think about anything else. Worse still, I didn't have a single answer, a single remedy.

And I was hungrier than ever.

ten

Day Three in Alba

The following morning, I was in the inn's lobby at 7:55 a.m. waiting for Luca, who'd said he was going to pick me up at eight.

Eight o'clock. No Luca.

Eight thirty. Still no Luca.

I called his cellphone. Straight to voice mail.

Nine o'clock.

Should I be worried? Should I be mad?

By nine thirty I went back to my room and called Luciana.

"I wouldn't worry," said Luciana. "He probably just forgot. He doesn't keep a calendar."

Really? You need a calendar to pick up your future business partner after agreeing to pick her up some twelve hours before?

"Or a watch," I added.

Either Luciana missed the sarcasm or chose to ignore it. "Rosa should be there later this afternoon to help you with the Trattoria Naturale paperwork, if that's okay with you," she said.

What on earth was I doing here? Suddenly it all felt like a waste of time. "Yeah, that's fine," I said.

A loud sigh broke away from me, as if it had a will of its own, after I ended the call. Stood up by a pasta troll. What were the odds?

With nothing else to do, I changed into workout clothes. What I really wanted, I realized, was to go for a run. But where? There seemed to be nothing but either hilly vineyards or narrow city streets as far as the eye could see. In a mix of Italian and English, I asked the concierge at the front desk the whereabouts of a nearby gym. He shook his head, but I wasn't sure whether it was because the answer was no or if he didn't understand me, even though he too spoke a mix of Italian and English. I wound up settling for multiple sets of squats, planks, and crunches on a bath towel in my room.

So unsatisfying.

————————

Almost three hours after my pathetic attempt of a workout, unintentionally falling asleep while reading a quarterly report, the clanging tintinnabulation reverberating from the landline assaulted my ears and shoved me out of a dream. Within seconds, my brain alerted me to the stiffness in my neck and lower back.

When I answered the phone—first with a froggy, frazzled "hello" and quickly correcting it to a more polite "*Pronto*"—the concierge's friendly voice informed me that Luca was waiting in the parlor. As if I'd stood *him* up! I went slack-jawed, completely baffled. "Tell him I'll be down in ten minutes," I said, and hung up, forgetting to say thank you. I pulled my hair into a ponytail, slathered on some lip gloss, slid into a pair of Keds, and entered the parlor as poised as I could be, despite looking around for something to bean Luca with.

"*Buona sera*, Miss Katie!" he said, all chipper and perfect and disgustingly gorgeous.

I was having none of it. "Do you know how to tell time? Did they teach you that in school along with your handsome lessons and soccer? Or were you sick that day, and missed it along with the tutorial on courtesy?"

I couldn't help but notice that he'd perked up for a split second upon hearing the word "handsome" (and dammit, why did *that* come out of my mouth?), but then he shrugged me off as if I'd suggested something ludicrous, like wearing a thong.

"You are in Italy," he said, "Land of leisure."

"No," I barked. "Don't give me that stereotypical Italian bullshit. You stood me up this morning, without even bothering to apologize. You decided that my time and respect was of no value to you. It had nothing to do with culture or lifestyle or anything. You were rude, plain and simple. I am not here on vacation, or to be leisurely." *Says the woman in workout clothes . . .* "I am here on *business*. I have important responsibilities to attend to, and cannot afford to have my time wasted by someone who wants my business to fail—an attitude, by the way, that is sure to send his own business down the crapper."

Why had I never said anything to Max when he cheated on me? Why had I never stood up for myself, told him what a fool he'd made of both of us, and Cheetah too? Why hadn't I told him that his behavior with me was sure to doom any possible future he had with her or anyone else, and that I had deserved better from him? Where had my voice gone that day? All I had managed to say was "Get out." And then I felt bad about it. *I* felt bad!

Luca stood in front of me, arms dangling at his sides, looking utterly bewildered.

And then, as if I was right back in my betrayed bedroom, I put a hand up as if to block Luca from saying anything, even though his mouth was clamped shut. "Get out," I said. *Déjà vu* all over again. "Get out of my sight."

He didn't move. After a suspended pause, he spoke softly, almost tenderly, even. "Have you eaten today, Miss Katie?"

You know how in the Road Runner cartoons when Wyle E. Coyote doesn't realize he can't defy gravity until he looks down midair and plummets? In that instant I felt a hunger pain so severe it made me woozy.

Next thing I knew, I was on the floor, in Luca's arms, my head in his lap, with a cool, wet towel on my head.

"Wha . . . what happened?" I slurred.

"You passed out," said Luca matter-of-factly.

"For how long?"

"Five to ten seconds, tops."

"You got a compress on me in ten seconds?"

"So maybe it was fifteen. I can't tell time, remember?" And with that he winked. He *winked*.

Shit.

I could hear his next line in my head: *I've had women fall for me before, but this is ridiculous . . .*

I tried to sit up, but Luca restrained me. "Gently, Miss Katie. Not so fast." He then helped me to a sitting position and handed me a piece of bread. "Take a bite," he instructed. "Chew slowly."

I nibbled on the crusty, broken baguette. It felt dry and flat on my parched tongue, albeit soft. Next he handed me a bottle of water, and I sipped and swallowed. Slowly, with intermittent nibbles and sips, the fog in my head cleared, leaving me with a head-to-toe ache.

"I shouldn't have worked out on an empty stomach and then fallen asleep," I said. "I know better. I'm just . . . I should be home. My company needs me. My . . ."

Who else needed me? I'd long stopped making time for friends, and they'd long stopped calling me to ask for it. My parents and siblings and I were never a Sunday-dinners-and-holidays kind of family. My younger sister was a professor at a New England university and seemed to travel from academic conference to academic conference like a groupie following a tour band. My younger brother lived in Portland, Maine, as a Starbucks barista and felt his life was complete. My parents, divorced since I was eighteen, lived in separate towns in Florida. They'd always had their hearts set on retiring there, and I guess they figured the state was big enough to accommodate both of them without them having to come in contact with each other. Mom kept busy with shuffleboard, knitting club, book club, garden club, and her annual Thanksgiving cruise. I'm not sure what my father did other than paint watercolor seascapes, but if they didn't live in a climate where your hair frizzed up even in the shower, I would have visited them more often.

I didn't even have a goldfish. Or a plant.

Luca helped me to a standing position, steadying me along the way and keeping a firm hand on my shoulder for support.

"It's okay, Miss Katie," said Luca. "Let me make you something to eat." He then said something in Italian to the concierge, who responded as obediently as I had when Luca handed me the bread, and led both of us into the kitchen. The concierge gave me a stool to sit on while Luca commandeered the kitchen, finding an apron and raiding the pantry and stainless steel fridge for ingredients: bread. Salami. Tomato. Basil. He then grabbed a skillet and set it on a low flame burner, and chopped the tomato with lightning speed. When the skillet heated, he drizzled olive oil into it.

"Always add the oil after the pan heats, not before," he said, as if I were his pupil. He then unfolded a thin slice of the salami—"soppressata," to be exact—and gingerly spread it across the skillet like a blanket on the beach. "We're going to sear this just for a few minutes to give it texture," he said. "We're not cooking it like bacon. More like a delicate fish." He'd just finished saying the words when he flipped it with both a spatula and his fingers.

"I love how instructors always say 'we' when teaching someone how to do something, even though they're doing it all by themselves," I said, hoping it didn't come out as a criticism. Rather, I found it amusing and, at the moment, even endearing. "Have you ever thought about doing a cooking show? I think you'd be a huge hit in America. You've got the—um, talent for it." *And the looks.* "And you've got the personality too. You're already sort of a celebrity in the pasta world. Why give Guy Fieri all the fun?"

In mid-slice he froze, his hands balled up, and he clenched the knife and slab of bread as if he were about to stab it *Psycho*-style. And then he launched into a tirade of what had to be Italian expletives, the only words I recognized being "Guy Fieri" between each one. You don't need to know the words or what they mean to know when someone is swearing up a shitstorm.

At first I recoiled in horror. But then, for the first time in I can't even remember, I laughed. Hard. And Luca wasn't even trying to be funny, that much I knew. But still.

"Okay, okay," I said, trying to calm him down. "I get it. Sorry I brought it up. I'm just saying, you'd be good at it."

"No self-respecting chef would parade around the country, selling out. It's a disgrace. An abomination. It stops being all about the food and starts being all about them. It should be about the *food*. It should always be about the food. *Il cibo è vita*," he said yet again. I knew those words by heart now. *Food is life.*

"Oh, come on," I said. "Tell me how that's different from what you do. I Googled you, you know," I confessed. "I've seen your press clippings. You get around. You make guest appearances in restaurants all over."

"Always to cook," he interjected. "Never to get my picture taken."

"Oh, so that just happens by accident," I said. "The cameras hit you on the way out."

"It's a by-product. I can't control it." He finished slicing the bread and toasted the slices directly over the flame in under a minute. Finally he assembled everything: the seared meat, the tomato, and basil on top, and drizzled the olive oil across in a manner that seemed equal parts reckless and precise.

He extended the plate—shiny with color and so delicately layered, like one fabric on top of another—and I leaned in and admired it.

I'd never witnessed food as something *pretty* before.

"Soppressata crostini," he said. "Appeals to your American sensibilities. Eat with your hands."

"I hope you'll join me," I said. "I hate eating alone. I especially hate when people watch me eat alone."

He rolled his eyeballs around and muttered as if I'd just nagged him to clean the garage, but he picked up a crostini and sunk his teeth into it with me, in synchronization. The flavors spread across my tongue—the saltiness of the soppressata; the bitterness of the basil; the tanginess of the tomato—and it was better than any triple latte or Vitamin B shot or multiple reps of crunches. By the time I finished two crostini, I felt alert. Invigorated. Awake. I felt *fit*.

I felt full.

Satisfied.

It was as if Luca Caramelli had just kissed me.

And before I could sink further under the spell, he broke it by announcing, "Tomorrow I teach you how to make pasta. It's time."

And for the first time not only since I'd arrived in Alba but also since Max and I broke up, I had something to look forward to.

eleven

Day Four in Alba

Either my body was finally adjusting to the time and routine change, or I was just plain feeling better. Maybe it was because I'd actually felt productive when Rosa came last night and helped me organize and understand all of Trattoria Naturale's paperwork. Or maybe it was because I ate breakfast upon waking this morning. Consciously. Willingly. Even mindfully. Hazelnut scones and raspberry jam and espresso. Every bite a manifestation of the sunny morning awaiting me outside the inn.

Regardless of the reason, I wasn't complaining—I was energetic and eager to get to work. Luca was—*gasp!*—right on time and waiting for me in the parlor, holding a basket covered with a linen towel. Figuring that things were going to get messy in the kitchen today, I dressed in workout clothes. Well, workout clothes and a full face of makeup.

He extended the basket. "I brought you breakfast, in case you forgot to eat again."

"Wow, that was thoughtful of you," I said, as if the concept of Luca thinking about anyone other than himself was a novelty. "And you'll be pleased to know that I already ate. First thing this morning."

He looked disappointed, actually.

He didn't move or say anything. I followed his lead. Finally, I broke the silence. "Ready to go?"

"Are *you*?" he asked. "You look like you're about to film a workout video."

I didn't know whether to be amused or insulted. "Let's go, Luca," I said, taking the basket from his hand and walking out to his car.

On the way to Trattoria Naturale, I pulled back the linen towel and peeked in the basket, finding hulled strawberries and biscotti. I popped a strawberry in my mouth. "Mmmmm, juicy," I said in mid-chew. My fingers fastened themselves to a second one. "Want one?" He shook his head. I popped that one as well, silently deciding to skip logging two strawberries on the Pasta Pronto food journal app.

"Try the biscotti," he suggested, and I acquiesced, breaking off a corner and tasting it. My entire mouth woke up.

"Ohmigod, it's so . . . *lemony*," I exclaimed. "And yet, it's neither too tart nor too sweet. Sorry, I know I sound like a bad commercial. But still."

"It's okay," he replied. "I'm glad you like it." He seemed unusually quiet.

"What does 'biscotti' mean in Italian?" I already knew the answer, but felt the need to engage him in conversation.

"Twice baked, or twice cooked. You make the dough, bake it in the oven, let it rest, and then bake it again."

"Who has time for that?" I asked.

"Who has time to drive all the way to the supermarket, push their cart up and down twenty aisles, and spend five dollars on a box of cookies made from chemicals?"

"Well, not me. But I don't eat dessert, so . . ."

"I don't get that," said Luca. "I mean, I know why you don't, but I don't . . . *get* it. I don't understand how you can deprive yourself of something so simple and pleasurable."

"Because it's neither simple nor pleasurable for me. Look, I'm not one of those people who can eat one little petit four and walk away. I want to eat, like, *forty* of them. And lick the plate. And then wash them down with a gallon of ice cream."

"Have you ever actually done that? Seriously, Miss Katie. Have you?"

The question transported me back to middle school when, at age fifteen, I went to my friends' slumber parties and we binged on Doritos and Devil Dogs and Häagen-Dazs and Diet Coke—as if drinking a one-calorie soda somehow absolved you of all your other sins—until we could hardly walk, resolving to go for a group run or work out to our mothers' Denise Austin videos the following morning, which we never did.

The bingeing was nothing compared to the shaming we all did immediately afterward:

"Ugh, I am such a pig."

"I know, right? Like, what boy would ever want to be with cows like us?"

"Never again. I'll die if I'm ever anything more than a size two. My mother just put my little sister on Weight Watchers."

But of course, the following weekend it was same crap, different girlfriend's house. Why? Why did we binge in the first place if we were just going to punish ourselves later?

"Look," I said to Luca. "It's not easy when you inherit your father's sweet tooth—and a salty one too, come to think of it—and your mother's disdain for it." In fact, my two younger siblings and I loved when our mother went away for a weekend and left Dad to do the grocery shopping. He'd come back with sugary cereals and Keebler cookies and instant pudding and Ruffles potato chips and Oreo Cookies and Cream ice cream with an array of sundae toppings and spray cans of whipped cream.

And steaks. Big ones.

"And it's not easy when your dad is the one they ask to play Santa Claus at the Y every year," I continued.

Thing is, he loved playing Santa. Dad was a good forty pounds overweight, and the only ones who had seemed bothered by it were Mom and his doctor. I had always loved resting my head on his soft belly when we watched cartoons together. Mom had nagged him constantly, however, and made him keep a record of everything he ate, pasted on the refrigerator for all to see. At least the Pasta Pronto app was private.

"*Don't treat me like a child*," he'd snapped at her one day from behind their closed bedroom door, outside of which I'd eavesdropped. "*It's my body and my life. I'll eat whatever I damn please.*"

"*You won't have any life if you keep eating what you damn please*," Mom had replied. "*Geezus, Henry—don't you want to see your children get married some day?*"

"*You make it sound like I'm obese. So I'm a little thick around the middle. That's what happens to men in their forties. And may I remind you that* you're *the one who used to cook and give me too-big portions and made me clean my plate so as to not piss off the starving kids in Ethiopia? You used to love to feed me, Janelle."*

"You're more than 'a little thick.' You're repulsive."

After what had seemed like hours of silence, my father had spoken so softly I could barely hear him. *"Your lack of libido has nothing to do with my waistline. You started withholding from me long before I gained a pound. For God's sake, why do you think I eat so much? I need something to fill me."*

And that was all my sixteen-year-old ears needed to hear.

I babbled on to Luca, seemingly unable to stop myself in the same way I couldn't stop at one potato chip or Mallomar: "And it's not easy when your parents divorce while you're still in high school and your mother strips every shelf of everything with more than a gram of fat in it and restricts you to a diet of rice cakes and boiled chicken."

My parents divorced after my father gained another twenty pounds. Years later, in my late twenties, I'd found out that my mother had had an affair. I'd figured it was because my dad was too *repulsive*, just as she'd said. And now, thinking about it all, I realized that I'd come to see him through my mother's eyes because she'd stopped saying it behind closed doors. He was fat. He was unhealthy. He was no longer handsome.

So I swore: I'd never be repulsive to anyone. Ever.

And thus ended any interest in cooking and began my vigilance with the scale.

We were not going to take after *him*, Mom had said. We were going to have to find different ways to fill ourselves. But boy bands and straight As and shopping at the mall with friends hardly filled the longing for my dad to come home, or a boy to take me to the prom. Spaghetti and meatballs somehow soothed me the same way a hug did. And sneaking cookies to my room after secretly buying them at the corner deli somehow gave me power over my mom's tyrannical control of the pantry.

Not to mention that some of my best moments with my father were when we shared a hot fudge sundae. Or when he took me out for pancakes on a Saturday morning. Or gave me a box of Sweethearts for Valentine's Day. And yet, I'd never associated our good time with the food; rather, I'd always remembered the *attention* he gave me. The way he smiled at me with such pride.

Whom did I resent more—my mother for being so restrictive with my father and us, or my father, for showing no restraint whatsoever?

Thing is, I took after both of them. When I founded Pasta Pronto, I thought I'd gamed the system. Found a way to have what my mother always forbid me and what my father was forced to give up when he was diagnosed with heart disease and high cholesterol. The "filling" part was running a successful company, and getting to eat pasta every day and still fit into my wedding dress.

Although what did it get me? I lost my fiancé to a woman who had no qualms about eating whatever she wanted. I had a wedding dress, but no wedding.

"And it's certainly not easy when your fiancé dumps you for a woman who eats . . ."

I finally stopped myself when my eyes had become wet and blurry. Realized what I'd revealed, put on a platter for Luca to devour. I didn't even realize that Luca had pulled the car over.

Luca caressed his thumb across my cheek, taking a tear with it, his eyes fixed on mine. Oh, his eyes, glistening like a starlit sky . . .

Wait, what?

Get a hold of yourself, Katie Cravens!

I pushed Luca's hand away and swept the back of my hand across my eyes to rub the tears away. No way was I going to succumb to kissing him when I was a raccoon-eyed hot mess. And I *wanted* to kiss him. Badly. And more. No way was I going to expose my weakness. Takeovers happened when companies—and their leaders—were vulnerable.

No. Way.

"Drive the car," I commanded, sliding away from him in the bucket seat and as close to the door as I could get without opening it and falling out.

Luca and his pheromones leaned back in his seat, but he didn't put the car in gear. Didn't say a word.

"Look, I'm sorry I suddenly went all blubbery on you, but can we just please go to the restaurant and get this over with?" I said, although at the moment I wanted to be in a kitchen about as much as I wanted to be in the car. Or in Alba. Or anywhere else that was neither my office nor the gym, where Power Katie was always in control.

Luca gaped at me in puzzlement as if I were a peculiar creature from another planet.

"Do you want to get back at your fiancé?" he asked.

I said nothing, waiting for his answer as if he were dangling an éclair on a stick in front of me.

"*Live,*" he said.

That's it?

"Live for *you*," he clarified, as if he'd read my mind. "Your entire life has been one of deprivation. You've been telling yourself what you *should have*, not what you *want*."

"I *wanted* Max," I snapped.

"No, you didn't. You wanted a husband and a house and three children because someone told you that's what you wanted. Fairy tales and television and magazines. Your ex-fiancé, he probably fit the mold perfectly. A lawyer in the right income bracket and still connected to his alma mater and hair shiny enough for a shampoo commercial."

What, had he *met* Max?

I stared at Luca, agape, unable to respond.

"Why are you blonde?" Luca asked.

My hand reflexively grabbed my ponytail and pushed my bangs away from my face. "What do you mean, why am I blonde? Of all the rude things to ask . . ."

"It's not your natural hair color." His tone added a silent "obviously."

"I . . . Blonde is more . . . Being blonde gets you things you wouldn't normally get," I said.

Luca shook his head. "That is complete and total bullshit."

My God. The word *bullshit* never made me horny before. It dripped off his tongue like donut glaze.

Luca reached over and, in one fell swoop, pulled the elastic off my ponytail and let my hair fall to my shoulders. "I want you to be *you*, Miss Katie. Not some freeze-dried, prepackaged, chemically concocted version of you, like the meals you manufacture. I want you to live on your terms. I want you to fall in love . . ."

He paused, letting the words dangle, teasing me, terrorizing me . . .

". . . with *food*. With life. With . . . yourself."

My heart sank.

"And then what?" I asked. "What does that get me?"

He locked me into a gaze and said with conviction, "Anything your heart desires."

twelve

When we entered the kitchen at Trattoria Naturale, Luca already had everything set up in twos: cutting boards, separated by a little glass jar of sea salt. Forks. Measured mixing bowls full of flour, eggs, and olive oil, respectively. Rolling pins. A box of plastic wrap.

After we washed our hands, Luca put on his chef's jacket and handed me an apron.

"So when do I get to wear one of those?" I asked, pointing to his chef's jacket.

I'd asked the question sarcastically, but he answered in a dead serious tone. "When you're ready for it." They were the first words we'd spoken since my car meltdown.

"I was kidding," I said. "I don't—"

"This is so easy you'll wonder why you never learned it before," Luca interrupted. "Watch me and do what I tell you to do."

"Yes, Chef," I said in mock obedience. Luca glared at me, but continued. He took the bowl of flour and dumped it on the cutting board.

Already I was perplexed. "We're not mixing it in the bowl?"

"A lot of people these days use state-of-the-art electric mixers and food processors. I'm going to show you how my grandfather made pasta. 'Old-school,' as you would say."

He motioned me to dump my bowl of flour on the cutting board, promising that next time we'd add semolina flour as well. Next, he picked up his fork and shaped the flour into a bowl by making a well in the middle. I tried to imitate him, but all I seemed to be doing was making fork indentations in the flour.

"Use your fingers," he instructed.

For some reason I felt as if I were a kid playing in a sandbox, although nothing about this felt fun.

Luca picked up two eggs and, one at a time, cracked and released their contents one-handed into the middle of the flour well. In response, I handled an egg and nervously smacked it so hard against the side of the cutting board it broke and splattered all over my hand.

"Shit!" I yelled.

Luca handed me a towel, and the more I tried to clean it, the more of a mess it became. I washed my hands again. Luca handed me another egg. "Try again. A little more gently this time."

My turn to glare. "Ya think?"

This time I was too gentle, daintily tapping the egg on the side of the board, until Luca impatiently took the egg, gave it one assertive tap, and broke it open into the center of the flour well.

"Have you never cracked an egg before?" he asked.

"This may surprise you, but I used to cook quite a bit during my adolescence, before—I used to make french toast for my siblings all the time," I said. And come to think of it, that may have been the last time I cracked an egg. Or, at least, that's how long it felt.

Luca stopped and looked at me, surprised. "Really?"

"My father taught me."

"Was he a good cook?"

I nodded, forcing myself to move the memory back to the depths of the freezer, where I'd repressed it long ago, before the emotion that came with it could catch up.

"Was your french toast good?"

"My younger brother and sister liked it."

I was expecting him to retort with something like, *They probably didn't know any better*, but he surprisingly smiled with delight.

"What else did you used to make?"

"Salads," I said in an attempt to stave him off the topic.

It worked. I could feel the burn of his skeptical stare. And as quickly as his demeanor inflated, it deflated and he redirected me back to the task. "Do the other egg."

This time, feeling more relaxed, I was able to crack and break the egg open with more precision.

"Okay, now add a generous pinch of salt to the well," he said. He seized the salt between his thumb and first two fingers and dropped it into the well with a spring in his wrist, as if making an exclamation point where a period belonged. I was less enthusiastic in my pinching. "And add the olive oil." He handed me a measuring spoon, but did his own straight from the bottle, measuring by sight.

"Are you going to tell me these measurements, or are they some Caramelli family secret?" I asked.

"Hardly. I'll write the recipe for you afterward," he replied. He clutched the fork again. "Okay, you're going to beat the egg a little bit"—he proceeded to do so without even disturbing the flour walls—"and then start pulling the flour into it, like this"—in a repetitive motion he pulled in some flour and beat, pulled in some flour and beat—"until it sticks to the fork and you take over with your hands." Rather than let me watch him follow the step all the way through, Luca instructed me to begin the process on mine. I began to beat the eggs with my fork. Immediately some of the egg spilled over the side of the flour wall. When I tried to push it back, the entire wall caved in and the egg overflowed, like water flooding a broken dam.

"Aghhh!" I yelped as I tried to block the runaway egg with the back of my hand. "Mayday! Mayday!"

Luca, with his hands full of sticky, half-mixed dough, cursed as he was forced to stop and rescue me. Somehow he managed to save the egg and reunite it with the flour, and then grabbed my hands and plopped them in the middle. "Just mix it," he barked.

I felt like I'd just had my hands dropped in cold, sandy Jell-O.

"Hey, I'm new at this, Chef Boyardee. Remember?" I bit back. "Cut me a little slack."

"Why should I?"

"Because there are two kinds of people in the world: those who make their own pasta, and those who don't. Those who make their own pasta also use a French press for their coffee and immersion blenders to puree soup and use words like 'umami.' Those who don't make pasta have jobs."

"I have a job."

"I mean jobs that keep them otherwise occupied."

He ignored both my pleas for mercy and my sarcasm. "Work it until it starts to solidify," he commanded. Within sixty seconds, Luca's egg-and-flour goop had turned into something not unlike the consistency of Play-Doh. "Knead it," he said.

I watched him in fascination, my hands glued in the slime pile, as he worked rhythmically, pushing the dough in with his palms, then folding and pushing again. Folding and pushing, folding and pushing, folding and pushing. Kneading, kneading, kneading . . .

Needing . . .

My God, his hands. His palms. His fingers.

Was it possible to be jealous of pasta dough? My neck desperately wanted to switch places. And my back. And my . . .

"Miss Katie!" he yelled, snapping me out of my fantasy. "Pay attention!"

"I can't! My hands are stuck! It's too . . . *blech*!"

He made a noise to communicate his exasperation, wrapped his supple ball of dough in plastic, and rubbed his hands together so fast the friction removed excess dough from his palms and fingers. I thought he was going to push me aside and finish for me, but instead he took hold of my hands as if they were utensils, making me pull the mixture together, adding a pinch more flour, and sure enough, the slime turned into something solid, forming right under my fingertips.

"Knead it," he said, now moving right behind me and placing his hands over mine, showing me how to use my palms the way he did. "Don't be afraid to get physical with the dough. Let it move to your will."

I could feel sweat beads forming at my temples as the temperature in the room shot up to one hundred degrees, or so it seemed. Luca's hands kneading my hands kneading the dough and his breath on the back of my neck fired my synapses on all thrusters. I couldn't even remember the last time Max had made me so hot. All I wanted was to turn around and run my dough-crusted fingers through Luca's silky hair as I kissed him, inhaling his spicy, delicious scent and tasting his lips and tongue and . . .

"Look how smooth and glossy and firm it is," said Luca.

"Stop it, will you?" I yelled, worming my way out of his grasp. "You are driving me *crazy!*"

Luca, startled, took a step back and watched me pant like a thirsty dog.

A Cheshire Cat grin appeared as he cocked an eyebrow. "I was talking about the pasta dough," he said. "Get it wrapped in plastic before it turns into a rock."

"Everything is sex with you, isn't it? It's not 'food is life,' it's 'food is *sex.*'"

Luca burst into laughter—that loud, raucous laughter that always made me feel two feet tall and want to crawl under the table.

I ran out of the kitchen and the restaurant—dough-crusted fingers and all—and hoofed down the street, trying to scrape the gook off by rubbing it on my yoga pants. *Perhaps I should scrape off the rest on his car. . . .*

Minutes later Luca caught up to me. "Where are you going, Miss Katie?"

"Back to Genoa—no, back *home*! I'll find some other way to save my company. No deal is worth this humiliation."

He jumped in front of me to block my path and pleaded, "Please don't go. I didn't mean to make you uncomfortable in there, and I certainly wasn't trying to take advantage of you. I know I am an asshole sometimes."

He stood contritely and looked at me with puppy eyes. And the thing is, I knew he wasn't being condescending, but rather sincere. "You don't deserve to be humiliated. Forgive me, please."

I scowled at him, and with my eyes said, *I'm forgiving you against my better judgment, but so help me if you pull this shit again,* and he got the message loud and clear.

Luca breathed a sigh of relief. "Thank you, Miss Katie. It won't happen again. Promise."

"I'll egg your car if it does."

He made an X across his chest with his finger. "Cross my heart."

"You know that expression?"

"I told you, I spent a lot of time in the States. Now, let's finish making our pasta."

"Fine," I said. "Whatever."

As we headed back into the restaurant, Luca said, without looking at me, "My Nonno would have loved you."

Nonno meant *grandfather* in Italian. And I knew unequivocally that Gianluca Caramelli had just uttered the nicest compliment anyone had ever paid me.

thirteen

The dough needed time to "rest," according to Luca. While it chilled in the fridge, Luca lectured me on the various pasta dishes in different regions of Italy, and how/why they differed from American pasta dishes. He spent fifteen minutes alone on the virtues of basil, noting that Italians don't come from a culture of mass-produced fruits and vegetables and herbs engineered for pesticide resistance rather than flavor.

"Your basil has no taste! No aroma!" he complained.

"Hey, it's not *my* basil," I said.

To be fair, "lecture" was too harsh a word. Luca spoke enthusiastically, passionately. His eyes were alight. His cheeks glowed. He gestured with his hands twice as much. Kind of like the way I acted when the bank approved of the Pasta Pronto business plan that had been my MBA thesis. And when I revived an abandoned factory in Hicksville, Long Island to manufacture the product. And when the first three Pasta Pronto meals—Linguine for Lovers, Perfect Primavera, and Guiltless Gnocchi—hit the local King Kullen and Waldbaum's supermarkets.

I absorbed as much as I could without taking notes. I didn't even know what kinds of questions to ask him. In that regard, Luca and I weren't much different. It's just that what excited us so much resided on opposite ends of the spectrum.

If Luca were a food, where would he rank on the Pasta Pronto color chart?

Orange. Definitely Orange.

As we talked, Luca prepared for the next step in Pasta 101—rolling pins, more flour, and saucepans full of water. He washed his hands and I followed suit.

"Okay, now we roll out the dough. We could use that machine over there—" He pointed to a shiny metal contraption with a crank handle locked onto the edge of a butcher block table—the pasta station, I assumed. The thing looked like some sort of vice grip you used to crush the fingers of workers who were rude to customers. "Even my grandfather used the machine toward the end, but first I want to teach you the way he taught me. It's just as effective, if not as efficient."

He dipped into the flour canister and sprinkled a handful onto his cutting board. As he repeated the gesture with the rolling pin, quickly, almost unconsciously, my mind conjured up a salacious phallic image as I watched him stroke it. *Ugh. Stop it*, I mentally scolded myself.

Luca removed the dough from the refrigerator and the plastic wrap, patted it with his hand a few times as if it were a pet, and began to flatten it with the rolling pin.

"Kind of like the scones the other day," I said.

"We're going to work it a lot more than that," he replied, not taking his eyes off the dough. I'd never seen anyone so focused on a task as Luca when he cooked. It was more than focus, though, and even more than determination. More like *devotion*, as if the kitchen were a church and the table an altar. But even that seemed too cheesy a description for Luca, one he would scoff at.

Could that have been me had I kept on cooking? Would I have become one of those chefs whose happiness out-girthed their waistlines?

One thing was for sure: I liked watching Luca work. I could watch him for hours, days on end.

He worked quickly, smoothing and thinning and elongating the dough.

"What kind of pasta are you making?" I asked.

"Fettuccine," he replied. "But you can make any kind of pasta you want with this dough—gnocchi, tagliarini, ravioli . . ."

Why does the Italian language make the words sound just as delectable as the food? Did we have words like that in the English language?

Buttercream frosting.

Yes. Yes, we did.

"I once had a boyfriend who went completely apeshit on me because I referred to pasta as 'noodles.' I swear, I think it's why he broke up with me. What's your stance on that?"

He paused and looked at me, as if noticing me for the first time, and gave me a look that said *How is it possible you made it this far in life?* I could feel my face flush with embarrassment—was his distaste in response to the "noodles" reference, that my ex-boyfriend found it to be a deal-breaker, or the fact that I brought it up in the first place? I honestly had no idea, and I didn't dare ask.

"Are you waiting for a formal invitation from me, Miss Katie?" asked Luca. "Roll out your dough."

"I think we should call your cooking show 'The Rude Chef,'" I said as I removed the plastic wrap from my softball-sized dough. "Only because you're not allowed to say 'asshole' on basic cable."

"Gordon Ramsay already has that market covered, don't you think?" he replied.

"Have you ever met him?" I asked.

"Once."

"And?"

"And he gave me a teddy bear. What do you want me to say, Miss Katie—that he screamed at me the moment we were introduced? We chatted for about ten minutes. He's a normal guy when he's not in front of a camera, just like anyone else, and a good cook. Precisely why I hate the whole celebrity chef thing and cooking shows and all that pomp. Don't forget to flour your surface and rolling pin," he tacked on.

"My aunt said she learned to cook thanks to Julia Child," I said. "There's nothing wrong with a show where people actually learn something. Not everyone has a famous chef grandfather."

I instantly regretted that last remark. Luca pressed his lips together tightly, and seemed to be fighting with all his might to suppress emotion as he continued flattening the sheet of dough with intensity.

"I'm sorry, Luca. I didn't mean—"

"See how thin it is?" Luca lifted his pasta dough and laid it over his fingertips to show me. "Like a fine fabric. That's what you want."

I observed his handiwork and nodded in comprehension before sheepishly returning to my own, working slowly.

"Keep rolling," he instructed, "but watch me too." He folded the dough with his fingers, forming a pencil-thin log and, with the knife looking like an extension of his hand, rapidly cut what looked to be quarter-inch strips. He then raked his fingers through and pulled the cuts apart and unfolded them and—lo and behold: fettuccine.

"Wow," was all I could muster. I looked down at my dough, still thick as a pancake despite all the rolling I'd done. He'd made it look so easy. My arms felt as if I'd done fifty reps with weights.

Luca filled a saucepan with water, set it on a burner, and turned up the flame.

"Faster, Miss Katie. You don't want the dough to dry out and toughen up on you."

I did as instructed, but rather than a long oval, my dough looked more pie-shaped. "Something's wrong," I complained. "It doesn't look like yours."

"Fold it," he commanded. So I folded the dough lengthwise, but when I rolled it out again, I now had a giant crease to contend with.

"Lucaaaa," I practically whined. "Hellllp meeee."

An impatient Luca muttered inaudibly and pushed me aside as he grabbed his own rolling pin and tried to fix my mistake.

"There," he said when he finished. "Now cut it into strips."

I grasped the knife—which felt like I could amputate a finger just by holding it—and sliced the first strip about a quarter-inch too thick.

"You don't *slice*, you *cut*. And you need to control your knife, not hold it like it's going to hurt you. Here—" He repositioned my palm and fingers around the handle and tapped my wrist. "See how that feels? Keep your wrist locked. Now, put the top part of the blade on the board above your dough, and bring the rest of it down like this." His hand still covering mine, he guided the knife over and through the dough gracefully and decisively, and repeated it several times so I could feel the rhythm. Knifework, I noticed, definitely had a rhythm.

Luca let go and let me take over, and by the time I finished, about a dozen strips of fettuccine in assorted sizes drooped lifelessly on the cutting board. In contrast to Luca's thin, pristine, okay—*pretty* fettuccine, mine looked like they wanted to be covered with a towel in shame.

Luca heated the second saucepan of water.

"We're not going to cook them all together?" I asked.

He shook his head. "I want you to see and taste the difference."

"I think you just don't want your noodles fraternizing with my noodles," I said. "Like wearing Prada and standing next to someone who's wearing, I don't know, Walmart." He rolled his eyeballs around, shook his head, and muttered again.

Both pots of water came to a boil. Luca pitched an ample amount of salt in each, dropped his fettuccine strips into the first pot in two handfuls, and instructed me to do my own. I held them by the edges and splashed them in one by one while his muttering persisted.

"At that rate the first one will be cooked by the time you drop the last one in. You're not dipping fondue."

"I don't want to burn my hand," I said.

"It won't kill you," he replied.

In the time it took for the pasta to cook, Luca placed a skillet on an open burner, drizzled it with olive oil, chopped three cloves of garlic in Flash speed, and added them to the skillet. He followed with chopped tomatoes, basil, and parsley, stirring them with a wooden spoon, and added his pasta to the skillet with tongs, not even breaking the strips. He then did that thing I've seen all chefs do on TV, which was toss everything together by shaking the pan a certain way—a jarring motion—without spilling a drop.

"Why not just mix it together with a spoon?" I asked. "Why be so show-off-y?"

"It's not to show off. It marries all the ingredients together. It's a different form of mixing."

"Don't you dare make me try that. It'll be all over the stove."

He gave it a few more tosses, then veered toward me. "You know, there's a difference between being a celebrity and being famous. Being famous means a lot of people recognize you on the streets or know you for something you've achieved, good or bad, regardless of whether you can help it or want to be recognized. Being a celebrity means you go out of your way to be recognized and get special treatment, regardless of whether you've achieved anything. My grandfather was neither. He was well-known and well-loved."

With the tongs, he clasped bouquets of fettuccine and set each one in spirals on the plate he'd set earlier, topping them with shavings of parmesan cheese and chopped parsley. "This is a more traditional American sauce, but it's simple." He extended a clean fork and spoon. "Taste it," he said.

"Say the magic word," I teased.

"*Now*. Before it gets cold."

"Not even close," I muttered.

I pronged one of the noodles with my fork and twirled it against the spoon. Then I brought it to my mouth.

Food orgasm!

I didn't even wait to finish chewing. "Oh. My God. Luca. So good. It's so light and . . . it actually tastes . . . *creamy*. And yet there's not a trace of milk or butter to be found."

Satisfying without the lingering effects of being full, I surmised.

I shoveled in more without paying attention to him making an identical sauce for my pasta. When he finished, he handed me yet another plate and fork and said, "Now taste yours."

Even though Luca applied the same presentation skills to my pasta, it didn't look anything like the pasta I'd just ransacked with every gluttonous, insatiable bite. I twirled my fork around again while Luca dipped his own fork in the plate at the same time, and we both tasted it.

Uck. If Luca's pasta was a food orgasm then this was . . . a misfire.

"It tastes . . ." I searched for a suitable word.

"Tough," he said.

"I was going to say *like shit*, but okay. Did you not cook it enough?"

"I cooked it precisely."

So, the problem was *me*.

"I mean, the sauce is good, but . . ."

"You'll get better at it," he said. Finally, some encouraging words.

"And you call this easier than dumping a bunch of boxed spaghetti into a pot or heating up a Pasta Pronto meal?" I asked.

"You'll never go back," he replied.

Nothing frightened me more than those words.

fourteen

I spent the rest of the day observing how the restaurant worked while trying to stay out of everyone's way—if I was going to help Alberto straighten out the finances, I figured I should know a little bit about what I was straightening. After bringing me the freshest arugula salad I've ever eaten, Alberto closed the door to the office.

"So what do you think of our little predicament?" he asked, knowing full well he was understating the situation.

"I think you need to start by getting a state-of-the-art computer and restaurant accounting software. Luciana can probably set you up."

Alberto shook his head. "I don't think that would be a good thing."

"Computerizing, or bringing in Luca's sister?"

"Both. Plus I don't know if we have the money for it." A pregnant pause took over, and I knew what was coming. "If you could help us out, Signorina Cravens . . ."

"Oh, Alberto, I'm very busy with my own company," I said apologetically. Before Alberto walked in I had been tending to whatever Pasta Pronto business I could long distance—approving the new cover art for our best-selling meals; discontinuing the Or-Zo Yummy Coconut Chicken dinner—too many bad memories attached; reviewing the latest batch of analytics during a conference call; signing off on employee evaluations; to name a scant few.

"I understand," he said. "Of course. I shouldn't have asked." His disappointment was poorly concealed. Alberto wasn't one to induce a guilt trip, but he was definitely feeling overwhelmed.

The guy got to me. I felt affection for him not so much as a big brother, but rather as an uncle. "I know you need help, Alberto. I'll do the best I can."

He kissed me on both cheeks.

In the kitchen, Luca was focused, albeit brooding. When he occasionally came out to the dining room to interact with customers, he was affable, even charming, although he always seemed to hold something back. The women seemed to be completely unaffected by his hotness, as if they'd been vaccinated with some kind of Luca-repellent. Maybe it was a regional thing, like not hearing what kind of accent you have until you go to another part of the country. I wouldn't mind getting a shot of it.

––––––––––––

Back at the inn in the middle of the night, I couldn't sleep. I kept replaying the day in my head: how I'd bared my soul to Luca about my parents, his hands on mine, kneading the dough, the smells and tastes of the kitchen, hearing Luca's voice saying the words *You'll never go back. . . .*

On the bedside table sat the basic pasta recipe written on thick vellum paper in Luca's handwriting—I didn't know people still wrote in script. I held it up to the beam of moonlight streaming through my window and read it as if it were more than a formula for fettuccine; rather, a formula for living. Maybe Luca's "food is life" chant was starting to take root.

The recipe was ridiculously simple. Two-thirds cup of all-purpose flour. One egg. One pinch of salt. One teaspoon of olive oil. That made one serving of pasta.

And suddenly, inexplicably, at 2:18 in the morning, I wanted to make some.

I crept downstairs to the kitchen—I didn't think guests were allowed, but given that Luca had so assertively allowed himself in there following my fainting incident, I figured I'd established a little clout-by-association. And besides, who would be there now, or find out about it if I kept quiet and cleaned up really well? Making pasta wasn't all that noisy.

It took a few seconds to adjust to the light when I flipped on the switch, but when I did I was able to find the ingredients I needed with ease, and, with a little drawer-and-door sleuthing, the equipment.

I followed the steps precisely and, as I recalled from the day, began with the flour well. This time my egg didn't run over the side when I beat it, but I must have mixed it all too quickly and wound up with a crumbly, grainy mess on the cutting board. I didn't want to add another egg, so I tried an extra teaspoon of olive oil to compensate, but then the dough got too wet and I went back to the flour to balance it out. The result was far from the smooth, shiny ball that Luca had kneaded twelve-plus hours ago, but eventually the dough conformed and I wrapped it in plastic.

What to do for thirty minutes?

I found myself looking for Instagram photos of Luca on my smartphone.

And then I found myself looking for Instagram photos of Max.

And I found them.

With Cheetah. And an engagement announcement.

Engaged.

My stomach lurched. My brain turned into a pile of rocks. My knees trembled. I grabbed onto the corner of the table to steady myself—if I fainted again, there would be no one to help me.

He and I were supposed to have been *married* by now. How? How did he get over me so quickly? What made me so easily forgettable and unlovable? How did he go from being certain *I* was the one to being certain *she* was the one so quickly? Had he gotten it wrong with me, or with her? And how on earth had I not seen it? What kind of fool was I, to be on the verge of marrying someone so fickle and be so oblivious to it? And to still be upset that I wasn't marrying him? Or rather, that he didn't want to marry me?

It hit me: you don't miss them when they're gone. Rather, you miss them when they move on.

Deep breaths, Katie. Deep breaths.

With five minutes still remaining, I removed the dough from the fridge, dumped a fog of flour on the cutting board and rolling pin, and began to furiously smooth out the pasta dough as tears silently slid down my face, one of them falling on the pin, another on the sheet of dough. Oh well. More salty that way. And the dough could use a little moisture.

Funny how much strength and speed you can acquire when you're pretending to flatten your ex-fiancé's face with a rolling pin.

I rolled the sheet of dough, now paper-thin, and cut into it, trying to make same-sized strips and untangling them to find assorted widths, and stopping midway to place a pot of water on the stove. By the time I finished cutting the strips, the water was on the verge of bubbling over. I dropped the doughy noodles into the water, letting it splash and prickle my arms as I watched the clear water turn into a sudsy, starchy white.

That's right, you little suckers. Drown in there.

Minutes later, I turned off the stove and impatiently picked up the handles of the pot to carry to the sink. However, my haste, coupled with my unfamiliarity of the kitchen, caused me to bump into the corner of the counter on the way to the sink and the boiling water sloshed.

And spilled.

Directly on my left foot.

I howled a fierce "FUCK!" as the water saturated my sock-covered foot and spread a blanket of pain across it, pain that moved up my leg and through my arms and settling right smack in the middle of my chest.

And yet, I stood there, immobile, my foot on fire, not knowing what to do first. Drain the damn noodles? Put the pot back on the stove? Tend to my sopping, burning foot?

Damn you, Max. If you were here right now, this water would be on your head.

The only solution I could come up with was to sit on the floor, clunk the pot next to me, and cry, coddling my wounded foot in my hands.

I was the CEO of a Fortune 500 company, and this was what my life had come to.

"What is this?" said the concierge. I looked up, startled. I didn't know those guys stayed on the premises.

"I . . . it's burned," I said, the humiliation smoldering almost as much as my foot.

He looked at the pot beside me.

"Not that," I said, and then held out my foot. "This."

I peeled off my wet sock to reveal an angry, molten splotch of red across the top of my foot, and the concierge's expression instantly turned from confusion to alarm as he spoke in urgent Italian. He helped me stand up and took me out of the kitchen and to the couch in the parlor, where he left me and returned moments later with a first-aid kit.

"I'm sorry," I said, as he gingerly applied an aloe-scented topical cream. "I swear I was going to clean everything up. I just wanted to make . . . I had a craving for . . . I'm just really sorry," I cried.

"It's okay," he said repeatedly as he elevated my foot onto an ottoman. I didn't know if he meant my foot was going to be okay, or if he was accepting my apology for destroying the inn's kitchen without permission. Several guests began to file into the parlor to watch him doctor my foot. Oh *holy frappe*, my expletive outburst must have woken everyone up!

He wrapped my foot in a gauze bandage and patted my ankle in a comforting way.

"It's okay, Katie," he said one more time. I didn't know he knew my name. Come to think of it, I didn't know his name. But at that moment, I fervently wished he were Luca. And I fervently wished even more that everything *was* okay.

fifteen

Day Five in Alba

I was still in bed when Luca knocked on the door at 10:00 a.m. After the concierge (his name was Giovanni, I learned) had taken care of my burned foot and cleaned my mess in the kitchen, I'd managed to fall asleep upon resolving to make a flight reservation and head home.

"Miss Katie?" I heard from the other side of the door.

I poked my head out from under the duvet. "Go away," I called out, and burrowed back.

"I'm going to break the door down if you don't open it."

"Please," I said. "These people here already hate me. Don't make it worse."

A pause. "I made lemon biscotti."

Lemon biscotti?

Damn.

I threw the covers off and hobbled to the door, temporarily suspending all care that I was un-showered, unkempt, and pretty much felt like death on a Triscuit.

That is, until I opened the door.

Goddammit, did Luca Caramelli ever not look like he was sculpted from marble? Did he ever have a bad hair day? Did he wake up perfect and preserved?

He entered the room empty-handed.

"I thought you said you had lemon biscotti," I said, following behind him and hoping he had a poor sense of smell.

"I said I *made* lemon biscotti; I didn't say I brought it with me."

I murdered him in my mind.

"Do you kick puppies too?" I asked. "I'll bet you do."

He spied my bandaged foot. "I heard about what happened. How is it?"

Oh God, had it made the local news or something? I sat on the bed. "How do you think it is? I've got a first-degree burn that's still smoldering."

"Why were you trying to make fettuccine in the middle of the night?"

"I don't know—because I felt like it, okay? Because I'm a crazy American girl with instant gratification issues and I wanted to get it right so I could prove to you that I also wasn't a stupid American girl."

His expression turned from apathetic to earnest in a heartbeat. "I have thought some things about you, Miss Katie, but none of them included stupid or crazy. Nor have I ever thought of you as a *girl*."

What did that mean, *I have thought some things about you*—what things? I knew he hated everything I stood for in terms of my company and went on the record saying so, but what else? I stared at him, perplexed, as if doing so long enough would unlock the key to his mind and enable me to read said thoughts.

Luca broke my trance. "Get dressed," he said.

I shook my head and crawled back into bed. "I'm not going to the trattoria with you today. Or ever again. In fact, I'm leaving Italy and going back to New York after I take this nap and book a flight. If you don't want to sign the contracts, fine. I'll go back and figure out another way to save my company. But I'm done here."

"Who said we're going to the trattoria?" said Luca.

"You're not working today?"

"I make my own hours."

I eyed him suspiciously. "Then where are we going?"

"You'll see. In fact, pack your suitcase."

I imagined Luca kidnapping me, bludgeoning me with a rolling pin, and dumping my body somewhere in the Mediterranean before getting rid of my stuff to hide all traces of me. The Pasta Troll becomes the Pasta Pronto Killer. There would be bad Lifetime Movie biopics and everything.

Were *those* the thoughts he had? I mean, sure, I got on his nerves and stood for everything he was against, but Luca wasn't the type. And he'd never want to make that kind of mess in his immaculate sports car.

Nevertheless, I voiced my ridiculous notions. "I'm a very important person," I said. "People will know I'm gone."

"Good for you," he said. "And them." He paused for a beat. "You should probably take a shower first. I'll wait." He sat in the chair by the window in the corner of the room.

Something about Luca in such close proximity to me while I was naked unnerved me even more.

"Wait downstairs," I said. Unfazed, he stood up and traipsed to the door. "And get me something to eat, please," I added. "I'm starving."

"Anything for a very important person," he mimicked, ostentatiously bowing in servitude as he closed the door behind him.

There had to be something I could electrocute him with.

I showered hastily, wondering what the secret destination was that required my packing. And come to think of it, *would* anyone know if I disappeared from the face of the earth? So far my company was getting along fine without me. My friends had written me off a long time ago, first for being too busy, then for being too Max-centered. My family didn't seem to care one way or another. And Max clearly had moved on.

An hour later, I entered the lobby with my luggage in tow. The shower had done me good and freshened me up, and Luca was waiting patiently with a tray of bread and berries and espresso, which I devoured.

"It's almost lunchtime; you should really eat something more substantial, but it's better than nothing," said Luca.

"So, am I checking out of here, or what?" I asked, on my third slice of bread.

"Well, you said you wanted to go home, right? Might as well." He was right. So why did my heart just sink?

"Did you leave anything upstairs?" he asked.

"No, I'm good. Just as well. I figured they were going to throw me out of here after last night."

No sooner than I said the words did Giovanni greet me warmly with a kiss on both cheeks. "Ahhh, *Signorina Katie*! How is your foot?"

Like it's being prodded with a thousand pin-sized hot pokers, thank you very much.

"It's better, I guess," I replied. "I want to apologize once again for invading your kitchen, and the mess, and—"

"It's fine, fine. We've enjoyed having you stay with us. You'll come back, yes?"

You'll come back??? Wow, the Italians were forgiving.

"Of course," I heard myself say, and I almost believed I would.

Giovanni and Luca exchanged what seemed to be pleasant-ries in Italian and then Luca took my bags and carried them out to the car.

"What about my bill?" I asked.

"Paid," said Luca.

"By whom?"

He pointed inward and poked his chest.

"But Luca . . ." I started, and then cut myself off. There was no way I could tell Luca that I was as concerned for his finances as Alberto and Luciana were, and that I had agreed to help out Alberto. "Thank you," was all I could muster instead. "I mean, *grazie*."

"*Prego*," he replied.

As we pulled away from the inn, a thought suddenly struck me. "Where have *you* been staying all this time?" I asked.

"In town," he replied. "My friend Ani has a room."

"That's nice," I said, wondering if I sounded every bit like the jealous lover I was failing to remind myself I wasn't. "You two known each other long?"

"Since we were kids. She was one of Luci's playmates."

I imagined all the games he played with Ani now: *doctor, librarian, boss and secretary. . . .*

"How sweet."

"So are her two little children," he added.

Wait, what?

My heart sprang into my throat, and I swallowed it back down.

"Yours?" I squeaked.

Luca guffawed. I turned as red as his Ferrari.

"I want to be a father about as much as you want to be a chef," he said.

My heart sank inexplicably again.

"I never said that," I said. "But watching you this past week, it's not so bad. I mean, I *could* learn if I really wanted to. To cook, that is."

"Do you want to?" He asked the question so sincerely it sent a shiver of fear through me.

"I . . . I don't know. Maybe I do."

Aside from not having the time to cook, not having anyone for whom to cook was the bigger obstacle. Cooking for one had always been a bore, pointless. Almost as lonely an endeavor as dining out (or in) by oneself.

But if that was the case, then why had I never wanted to cook for Max? Why had he never asked me to?

"Why don't you want to be a dad?" I asked.

"I don't think I have anything to offer a child," he replied.

"How can you say that? You're brilliant in the kitchen. You come from a strong family unit. You—"

He cut me off. "I'm just not suited for it. I'm too self-centered. I know I am. I want my freedom and I'm okay with that."

"Your parents don't pester you for grandkids?"

"They pester Luci."

"Typical," I said, but hastily apologized lest he think I was criticizing his parents. He didn't seem to care.

"I don't know if I want kids," I said after a pause.

What was I saying? Max and I had talked about having kids. I'd take a leave of absence from Pasta Pronto, he'd take a leave of absence from the firm, and we'd be a happy family, spending quality time nurturing our baby in his/her formative months. A year or two would pass before I had another, and Max would take another leave of absence and be a stay-at-home dad.

But what was it that Luca had said about my being sold on certain ideas? Wanting the picture of what I thought life was supposed to be like as opposed to the life itself? And whose picture was it—mine or Max's? In all likelihood, this plan probably would have been shot to hell. No way would I have wanted to leave my position, and no way would Max have left his. Gullible once again.

Ever since Max cheated on me and left, I could no longer trust a single thought I had. And it pissed me off to no end.

Luca didn't respond. Neither of us said a word for several miles. Unable to take the silence anymore, I piped up, "So are you finally going to tell me where we're going, or are we going to play Twenty Questions as a way to simultaneously pass the time and make me guess?"

"Genoa," he said. "Back to the villa."

"What was so secret about that?"

"Who said I was being secretive?"

I became agitated. "Then why didn't you tell me when I asked earlier?"

"Because I didn't feel like it."

"How old are you, Luca?" I asked. "Because you act about twelve."

"You did your homework—you know how old I am."

He was right, dammit. I already knew. Thirty-six. Same age as me, approximately six months my senior.

I shook my head, exasperated and weary. "I'm tired," I blurted.

"Close your eyes," he said, more as a suggestion than a command. I was in no mood to argue or be defiant, so I did. And then I heard Luca's voice, in soft, soothing tones, *singing*.

A lullaby. He was singing an Italian lullaby. I was sure of it. And in perfect pitch too.

No one had ever sung to me before.

He finished one and began another. Sure enough, his serenading swept me away to slumber. And just as I drifted off, I could have sworn I felt Luca's hand on my hair, stroking it once.

sixteen

We were back in Genoa when I awoke. I had yet to experience the scenery between the two cities; like being put to sleep in the Batmobile so as not to learn the secret location of the Batcave. Luca took my luggage out of the car and headed toward the villa, me following behind him and stretching my arms and legs along the way. Luciana wasn't yet home, which meant we had the place to ourselves.

Luca left my suitcase and his duffel bag in the foyer and made a beeline for the kitchen, raiding the fridge first and the pantry second.

"What are you making?" I asked.

Just like my first day in the restaurant, he prepared an antipasto course—prosciutto, black olives, cherry peppers, and provolone cheese combined with olive oil and the brine of the olives.

My fascination watching Luca cook was turning into more than just an appreciation thing. He was *sexy* when he cooked. Damn.

He placed the bowl on the table along with two salad plates, forks, and cloth napkins, and I helped myself. I began spearing the olives and relocating them to the napkin.

Luca gasped in horror. "What are you doing?"

"Picking out the olives."

He blinked in disbelief. "Why?"

"Because I don't like them."

He threw his hands in the air, signaling the start of another tantrum. "*You don't like olives?* What kind of person are you?"

"The kind who thinks olives suck."

"I don't understand this. It's . . . it's *wrong*," he said, looking like I'd just killed his cat.

Now I was egging him on. "Olives: pure evil."

Luca narrowed his eyes. "These aren't from a can or a jar, you know. They're real, fresh, un-chemicalized olives. You need to try them."

"I've had 'real' olives before," I said, gesturing quote marks with my fingers.

"Really?" he asked as he folded his arms, leaning against the counter. I tried not to be derailed by his pecs.

"Yes, really."

"And?"

"And . . ." *And they still sucked.* "And they were different. Besides, what does it matter whether they're fresh or come from a jar?"

Of course I knew the answer. And I knew Luca's answer. But I was having too much fun getting him all riled up.

"It matters!" he yelled.

I proceeded to remove another one, and he sprang forward as he threw his hands up again. "Stop it! You're ruining the meal! Like removing a heart from the body! They make food sing!"

"They make me gag," I replied.

"I demand you eat one of these olives right now," he said.

"You're not the boss of me."

"What is it, the saltiness? With all that sodium you put in those frozen abominations of yours . . ."

I rolled my eyeballs around. "Here we go again. You really like that word, don't you."

"Or is it the squishiness?"

"It's the squishiness. And the sliminess. And the sourness," I said matter-of-factly. "It's a trifecta of ick."

Luca popped an olive into his mouth and made a swooning noise. I knew that noise. Food orgasm. He was having one over *an olive*. Please. Why waste a good food orgasm on *that*? Then he darted his eyes at me angrily and said something in Italian that probably translated as "classless olive hater."

"If it makes you feel better, I love the prosciutto," I said. "I could eat prosciutto all day." Forgoing the fork, I seized a hefty cube with my fingers and popped it in my mouth the way he popped the olive.

For one second Luca seemed to consider this admission as redemption, but changed his mind the moment I added, "The olive brine kinda ruins it, though." He then snatched my plate and the antipasto bowl away from me and took them to the counter.

"What are you doing?" I asked.

"You don't deserve it."

"Seriously? You're punishing me?"

"If you're going to destroy my beautiful creation, yes."

I huffed and crossed my arms. "Fine. What's next?"

Luciana had made ravioli earlier, and Luca dropped them into a pot of boiling water. Next, he went to the window box housing an herb garden, ripped a heaving handful of basil leaves, and dropped them into a food processor. To that he added olive oil, pine nuts, cloves of garlic (which he'd chopped in the time it took me to blink), salt, and pepper. All the while he muttered in Italian, throwing eye daggers at me as he did, his expletives increasing in volume, and I knew he was still going on about the olives. He pulsed the processor and removed the ravioli practically at the same time.

Superman. He was Superman in the kitchen. If only I could figure out what his Kryptonite was.

Again he set two plates for us, this time filled with four humongous ravioli and shiny pesto sauce. "It's the same basic pasta recipe I gave you, only Luci adds semolina flour and sifts the all-purpose flour, as is customary. The recipe I gave you was for beginners. In time you'll learn the better way."

"What's in the ravioli?" I asked.

"Ricotta, romano, and fontina cheese," he answered. "My twin sister makes her own ricotta."

"No meat?"

He gave me such a dirty look that I swear had he been clutching a knife at that moment, he might have considered plunging it into my chest.

"I'm just asking!"

"Do you know what kind of sauce this is?" he asked.

"I'm not an idiot, Luca. I know what pesto sauce is. Pasta Pronto has a great linguini and pesto dish: we call it 'Presto Pesto.' Two hundred and seventy-five calories. It got top picks in a *Woman's Day* magazine poll."

"Impossible," he said.

"I can Google it and show you on my phone," I replied.

"No, impossible two hundred and seventy-five calories."

"You're saying I'm lying to my customers?"

"Either that or someone is lying to you."

Pasta Pronto had always faced criticism regarding our low calorie counts, especially following the food packaging scandal. Both our food scientists and lawyers assured me they were on the up-and-up since day one, which I staunchly explained to Luca. But what if they were lying to me? I'd been gullible enough to believe Max wasn't cheating on me. I'd been gullible enough to think I could persuade Luca to sign a stupid contract, and here we were, five days later. Up until this week, I had prided myself on being a savvy CEO, creating a company and a brand with the aid of trustworthy people who were very good at what they did. I had taken advice from one of my grad school mentors: if you're not the smartest person in the room, then surround yourself with people smarter than you. If you are the smartest person in the room, then surround yourself with smart people who disagree with you.

What if I had surrounded myself with the wrong people? I could no longer trust my judgment when it came to love. If I could no longer trust my judgment when it came to my work, where would that leave me?

I shuddered with fear, but refused to give Luca the satisfaction of my doubt.

I didn't need to. He shook his head and *tsk tsk*ed me. "Poor Miss Katie . . ." he said. "It's not your fault. I know how you Americans love to believe your fairy tales. Calories are not your enemy. Pasta isn't your enemy. It's thinking you need to sacrifice something in order to have a little pleasure. Calories, flavor, fat, salt, time . . . Olives were not meant to be in a can. Pasta was not meant to be in a box with plastic coating. It's unnatural. Haven't you learned anything these last few days?"

Screw sexy. Now I was mad.

"I learned that people are not meant to be treated like they're imbeciles," I said. "Luca, I have an MBA from Hofstra University. I am a woman who founded and runs a successful food company. I've received recognition from my peers for my business model. So I was raised on spaghetti sauce from a jar and I liked Pop-Tarts instead of . . . actual tarts. I also like sunsets and walks on the beach, learned how to knit a sweater when I was fifteen, and can dance the tango. I think it's about time you start paying me a little respect."

And with that I grabbed the bowl of pesto ravioli, along with my fork, napkin, and a bottle of wine that he'd set out at the start of the meal, and carried it all to the room I'd stayed in when I first came to Genoa.

The ravioli and pesto was outstanding. Of course.

seventeen

There are two kinds of people in this world: chocolate lovers and chocolate haters. Chocolate haters are usually the ones who refuse to encourage their kids to believe in Santa Claus and think the moon landing was faked and are deemed mentally incompetent to stand trial. Chocolate lovers are a fairly homogenous group, with the exception of the connoisseurs, who will tell you exactly where to place the chocolate on your tongue to get the full flavor effect and can recognize the cacao bean's country of origin with one whiff. Those people are weirdos. You know where I get the full flavor effect? *In my entire mouth.* When I see chocolate, I become a Pavlovian dog, dropping my jaw and panting for it, drool forming at the corners of my lips. My eyes bulge, my heart rate quickens, my entire body tingles.

Chocolate versus sex—has any scientist done a study to determine which one really is better, which stimulates the brain impulses more, fires more synapses, brings you to a better orgasm, leaves you more satisfied? Because they should. I would totally volunteer myself for such a study. For either group.

It had been quite a while since I'd last eaten chocolate. Or had sex. Forget about burning my foot. It was a wonder I was still speaking in complete sentences.

I was getting the hang of siesta. Sort of. I finally sorted through and organized all the paperwork for Trattoria Naturale after polishing off the ravioli in my room and three Dixie bathroom cups of wine. I pushed everything to the far edge of the bed, propped up a pillow, leaned back, and closed my eyes. Minutes later, I was prodded awake by some unknown force. Except the room was near dark.

Hang on. Not minutes later. *Hours.* I conked out for three hours. This on top of the nap in the car on the way to the villa.

Had someone knocked on the door?

"Luca?" I called out tentatively.

Silence.

I hopped off the bed and padded to the door and opened it to peak out into the hallway.

Empty. More silence.

He's probably in the kitchen talking to Luciana.

I continued down the hallway to the staircase. Most of the unoccupied room doors were left wide open. However, when I came to the end of the hall, the last door on the right was slightly ajar. I could hear a faint rustling, like crinkling paper.

Curiosity getting the best of me (and proper manners going completely AWOL), I stealthily edged the door open.

The glint of orange registered first. And then, gradually, the rest of the image formed and focused, and I could barely believe my eyes:

Luca Caramelli. Sitting on the edge of the bed. Eating a Reese's peanut butter cup.

No, not eating it. *Savoring* it. Eyes closed. Prolonged chewing. Holding the yet-to-be-consumed second cup, still in its wrapper, delicately between his thumb and forefinger. Making soft cooing noises.

I gasped and gaped and pointed my finger at him accusingly. "*You . . . !*" was all I could articulate.

Luca's shoulders jerked as he was startled—*coitus interruptus*—and panic paralyzed his entire body.

Finally, victory was mine! Luca had a weakness. A guilty indulgence. Kryptonite. And I intended to exploit it for all it was worth.

"You *hypocrite!*" I said with a villainous laugh, and plucked the pleasure source from his hand. "Look what we have here! Why, it's a Reese's peanut butter cup! But wait, that's not all! It comes in a wrapper! It's *processed!*"

Luca burned with humiliation, which only fueled my roast. "Refresh my memory—what farm grows Reese's peanut butter cups? Or do they come from the Reese's goat? Shall we read the abominable ingredients out loud?"

"Enough, Miss Katie," he snapped.

"Mister Food-is-Life, Mister Pasta-Pronto-is-Microwave-Bastardization, Mister Olives-from-Cans-are-Sacrilege . . ."

"*Chiudere!*" he shouted, his voice sharp and even a little shaky. I knew that word. It meant *shut up*. His gaze shifted from me to the Reese's.

I raised the remaining treat. "Oh, do you want this?" I taunted, waving it back and forth and watching his pupils follow it like an infant mesmerized by shiny keys. I then switched to Puppy Talk voice: "Come get the peanut butter cup! Come on! That's a good boy!"

Without warning, Luca sprang from the bed and lunged at me, gripping my hand with the remaining Reese's and accidentally stepping on my burned foot in the process. I yelped and fight-or-flight kicked in as I deflected his grabs and wrestled for control of the package being crushed between my palm and fingers.

In a matter of seconds, Luca pushed me back against the wall, pinning me there. I could smell his earthy, organic scent mixed with Reese's on his breath as I resisted and tried to break free from his grasp, until our eyes locked.

Primal. Wild. Fierce.

And then his mouth was on mine.

Good God, his tongue tasted like chocolate and peanut butter. Two great tastes that go great together.

My hand released the squished candy and went straight for his hair, which I'd been dying to run my fingers through since the day we met. Some of the chocolate had melted on my fingers and was now being combed through his hair like pomade. It felt so good to give in and let go, to stop thinking and let raw instinct take over. Luca's firm body pressed mine to the wall as he kissed me hard, heat escalating, both of us making yummy sounds, his hands running along my waist and around my hips and gripping my thighs, so close to a boiling point . . .

A voice called out. "*Luca!*"

Luciana. She was home.

Startled for the second time in mid-ecstasy, Luca abruptly abstained and unglued himself from me. The two of us panted loudly, frustrated, as my heart pounded with fear that Luciana was about to walk in on her twin brother and new business partner and find them—er . . . cooking together.

My back still pressed against the wall, I finger-brushed my hair and fanned my face with a clammy hand. For once my foot was the only part of my body that didn't feel like it was on fire.

"Luca?" Luciana called again, the sound of her voice drawing closer as she ascended the stairs.

"Go," Luca whispered, agitated, still taking short, fervent breaths, adding, "Hurry."

I slipped out, stepping on the peanut butter cup along the way, and crept down to my room in record pace, closing the door and leaning against it.

Holy frappe, what the hell just happened in there? How did it run off the rails so quickly? *What was I thinking?*

Oh. That's right. I wasn't thinking. Dammit.

I had strict rules about getting personally involved with people I worked with. Rule #1: DON'T. Rule #2: See Rule #1. I rarely even went out for drinks with any of my associates unless it was business-related. Perhaps it was the downside to being the boss. I simply didn't want to be put in the position of giving (or withholding) someone special treatment because of an emotional attachment. And that was just on the platonic level. Never mind sex.

This was bad. This was really bad. Luca was about to become a partner in a new product line. Sure, he wasn't going to have any public affiliation with it, and he'd be here and I'd be in New York, but still.

He'd be here and I'd be in New York. Let's just ruminate on that one a little longer.

Get it together, Cravens.

I heard the muffled voices of Luciana and Luca chattering away as I put my hand to my forehead and pinched my temples when I got a whiff of chocolate, and found the melted remnants on my fingers. Lovely.

I'm ashamed to admit I considered licking them.

Suddenly I felt three thumps on my back and I let out another yelp before I registered it as a knock on the door, followed by Luciana's sweet voice: "Katie, are you okay? It's Luci."

I stepped away, took a deep breath, turned around, and opened the door. "Hi!" I said, my voice up three nervous octaves. "So nice to see you again!"

Luciana gave me a curt but hospitable hug—I avoided touching her with sticky chocolate fingers. "Welcome back," she said. "I had no idea you'd be here today."

"I think your brother wanted a change of scenery. Plus I think my work here is done. I really need to get back to New York." My voice quavered as I spoke.

"Well, you'll need to stay for at least one more day so we can catch up and make plans and seal the deal, as you Americans say."

Seal the deal??? Oh. Right. The contracts. Sign the contracts. Lawyers on both continents had been drafting and negotiating for weeks.

A slow, silent panic began to bubble up. In one ear I heard my executive advisors telling me how this collaboration would be good for the Pasta Pronto brand as well as the coffers. In the other ear I heard whisperings that the Caramellis' coffers could use a little padding as well. And after seeing Trattoria Naturale's books, I understood why. A third voice—screaming from within—told me to get the hell out: of the villa, Genoa, Italy, and the Caramellis' lives. Together the voices swam about the squishy parts of my brain and made me go woozy and wobbly.

"Yes. Okay. Sure," I said.

She narrowed her eyes slightly. "Are you not feeling well?"

I looked at her blankly. "Fine. I'm fine. I burned my foot."

Luciana did a double-take. "*Scusami?*"

"Last night. Or early this morning. The middle of the night. I spilled boiling water on it." God, it seemed so long ago, although suddenly my foot started throbbing. I waved my hand dismissively. "Don't ask. It was stupid."

"Do you need a doctor?"

"No, I'm fine. The concierge at the inn took care of me. But I really do need to leave. I mean, I'll stay tomorrow, but then, you know. . . . This was good, though. Thank you. For everything."

She seemed dubious. "Okay. If there's anything you need, just ask me or Luca. I'm going downstairs to fix us supper. I'll have Luca call you when it's ready."

"Oh, no, thank you, I'm really not hungry."

In fact, I was ravenous.

She put her hand on my shoulder in a matronly manner. "Miss Katie, you need to eat. Please."

Her calling me "Miss Katie" jarred me. I didn't like hearing it from anyone but Luca.

I smiled to placate her, and she returned the smile and exited my room.

Just as I was about to close the door, a hand appeared and blocked it.

I recognized those fingers. Luca's.

My entire body simultaneously tensed and shook and tingled and went aflame like a stovetop burner.

"Miss Katie?" he said softly, as if testing the waters.

I backed away from the door as he let himself in. "Keep your distance, Caramelli," I said, uncertain where the sudden idiomatic use of his last name came from—I wasn't the type for such things—but I liked the empowering feeling it gave me. Like wearing Wonder Woman's bullet-deflecting bracelets. And I was good with accessories.

"I just wanted to tell you that my sister is going to make supper. Should be ready in an hour or so."

He still had flecks of chocolate in his hair.

"Yeah, she told me. About the supper."

We stood there and faced each other like two turtles in a staring contest.

Luca opened his mouth, but nothing came out. Epochs later, he tried again. "So . . . your foot is okay? I'm sorry for stepping on it."

I dropped my head to look at it. "It's fine."

He was about to say something else when I put up a hand to block it. "Luca, this can't happen, okay? We're in business together, and it was inappropriate. I apologize for my behavior. All of it."

His mouth clamped shut, and he wore the expression of a little boy who'd just been yelled at for messing up his mother's flower garden. Once again I imagined a young Gianluca, at grandfather Vincenzo's side in front of the stove, devoutly and adoringly watching him stir tomato sauce.

"It won't happen again," said Luca, his voice lowered in register, speaking like a professional. "My apologies too."

"Thank you."

The turtle stares were back.

Luca turned and left the room, closing the door softly.

I knew I was going to have to lock that door when I retired for the night. I wasn't sure whom I trusted less—Luca, or me.

Me. Definitely me.

eighteen

Awkward.

That's how the morning and afternoon went as Luca and I tried to ignore the fact that we'd come this close to a different kind of merger some fourteen hours ago. Luciana either pretended to be oblivious to the tension or really was as she conversed with both of us while still maintaining her plucky demeanor. And yet, when the lawyers came and we all congregated to sign the contracts, she was straight-up business.

Luca signed the contracts with no fuss. In fact, he didn't say a word.

For the first time since arriving in Italy, I exhaled a sigh of relief. My persistence paid off, and I'd gotten what I wanted all along: the contracts with Luca's signature.

But at what cost?

The ambitious side of me had expected to gloat. To do a victorious fist pump. This was a real coup for Pasta Pronto.

Instead, I called Wendy Blount and instructed her team to move forward on the press release we'd already drafted, as well as create some kind of public relations event to promote the partnership and new "A Taste of Genoa" product line.

Business as usual. It was simply one more completed task that spawned a thousand new tasks.

I did, however, buy a bottle of champagne and made sure it was delivered at the precise time of the signing so we could toast the occasion. Luci was appreciative of the gesture. Luca was cordial, at best, albeit quiet.

Rosa made travel arrangements for me. A car was going to take me to the airport the next day.

I should have been champing at the bit to leave. So why did I feel like there was something important I was forgetting to do? Why did things feel so unresolved?

During siesta, I changed into workout clothes and was planning to do some yoga poses outside when I found Luca wheeling two titanium bicycles out from the detached garage.

"You and your sister going for a ride?" I asked in what sounded like forced friendliness.

"Actually, I was about to invite *you* for a ride. It's beautiful countryside around here."

Don't do it, Katie. He's going to take you to some secluded area and you're going to wind up making love under a big oak tree. Or in a lake. Or . . .

"Sure. Okay," I said.

This is why you color-code your food. No willpower.

The only bike I'd ridden since attaining my driver's license at seventeen years old was stationary, but how hard could it be? After all, where do you think the expression "it's just like riding a bicycle" came from?

Whoever came up with that expression *lied*.

I wobbled all over the pebbly terrain while Luca effortlessly pedaled and coasted down the driveway path and onto the narrow road.

"Luca, slow down!" I called out from behind him.

"Keep up, Miss Katie!" he called back.

Ugh. Italian asshat. What in the world made him so attractive to me?

Well, his ass, for one thing, of which I had a nice glimpse from this vantage point.

I pumped the pedals as if I were at the gym, trying to think of a good workout song in my head. Nothing. But I was already working up a sweat.

Luca released the handlebars, extending his arms to the scenery, and shouted, "Isn't it beautiful!? *La vita è belllllllaaaa!!!*" he sang in Leonardo DiCaprio, I'm-king-of-the-world style and broke into a loud, carefree laugh before retaking hold of the handlebars and pedaling faster.

He wasn't wrong about the beauty, though. Rolling hills, clear skies with billowy clouds, vineyard rows, wildflowers, green, green, green. Light years away from skyscrapers and boardrooms and test kitchens and food labs and conference calls and treadmills and balance sheets and iPads and shareholders and gridlock and . . . and . . . *control*.

Which is exactly what I lost when a cat darted across the road to beat a car barreling in the opposite direction. I shrieked as I swerved around the cat and then the car and careened off the road and down a hill and flipped over, where I rolled and landed in a stream. A very shallow stream, but nevertheless, a stream. As in wet. And cold. And muddy.

I managed to balance to my knees before standing in ankle-deep water, my sneakers sloshing as I stepped onto mossy land.

Luca, realizing what had happened, circled around, parked his bike at the top of the hill, hopped off, and galumphed toward me. "You okay, Miss Katie?" he asked.

My knees and elbows were scraped. My shoulder hurt. My foot stung.

He repeated the question.

I stood there, every part of me throbbing and aching and soaking, and looked at him.

And then I screamed.

Long and shrill and echoing, it rattled Luca as he cringed and covered his ears.

And then I ran over, took hold of him, and shoved him so hard he fell and rolled into the stream as well. He jumped to his feet and yowled expletives as he wrung out his shirt, exposing his abs underneath.

I exhaled a long, satisfied breath. "Now I'm okay," I said, and stumbled back up the hill, retrieving the mangled bike along the way and wheeling it back to the road.

Luca followed me. "Was that really necessary?"

"Yes. Yes, it was."

He caught up to me, his eyes ablaze with anger, and I thought he might slap me.

Instead, to my complete surprise, he broke into laughter, which immediately infected me, and I could actually feel the aches and burns and stings floating out of my body and into the ether as I cracked up. That's exactly what it felt like—cracking up. Going mad. Finally succumbing to the absurdity of it all. And not just the last six months of my fiancé cheating on me or my company on the brink of collapse and buried under lawsuits. No, it was the absurdity of every counted calorie, every weighted carrot, every crunch and plank and lunge devoted solely to keeping me in a size two. And what the hell was a size two, anyway? What did it mean when you were alone and standing in the most beautiful place on earth, soaking wet?

Luca, the ends of his hair damp and a scratch on his cheek, grinned and said with more warmth than I'd ever heard from him, "Let's get you home, Miss Katie."

We walked the bicycles back to the villa, laughing and bickering all the way. I couldn't remember the last time I felt so alive.

Hours later, after a decadently soothing, hot bath, I caught a glimpse of myself in the mirror and saw myself transformed from ragged, stressed out Katie to softer, calmer Katie. Giving my body yet another once-over, I tried to picture the reflection of a heavier version of myself, not unlike the teen and young adult I had been. Max had once joked— and I didn't believe his jocularity for a second—that he would divorce me if I got fat. And yet, Cheetah had a good twenty to thirty pounds on me.

What was it all for? Why had I devoted my entire life to making sure my body looked and felt a certain way? Sure,

Pasta Pronto touted a healthy lifestyle, but were I to be really honest, I wasn't enduring those yoga poses and reduced calories to maintain a healthy heart. No, I wanted to ensure that whoever laid eyes on my body would desire it for themselves. If they were female, then I wanted them to desire it with envy. If they were male, then I wanted them to desire it with lust. But so far the men I'd met in Italy seemed to be unaffected, actually commented that I could use more, not less flab. And body-type made no difference in leadership or problem-solving skills or when it came to Pasta Pronto or my efforts to help Alberto get his restaurant back in the black.

I was suddenly tired of looking at my body. Tired of inspecting every inch of it and calling out every imperfection. Tired of caring about it. Perhaps I should start paying more attention to a healthy heart. And I didn't only mean the muscle.

I changed into pajamas and descended to the kitchen for supper. Luca was there, but nothing was simmering on the stove or baking in the oven or cooling on the counter. He just sat at the table, a glass of wine in his hand, and stared wistfully into nothingness until he saw me, and his eyes widened and lightened.

"Feeling better?" he asked.

"Tons," I replied. "I'm taking those bath salts home with me. Outright stealing them."

"I'm sure Luci will have no problem with that."

"Where is she, anyway?"

"At the restaurant." He took another sip and then showed me the glass. "Prosecco?" he asked.

"Sure," I replied. He pulled the empty glass on the table to him, poured, and set it at a place for me, where I met and brought it to my lips. Sweet.

"So what's for supper?" I asked more coyly than I'd intended.

He gazed at me in such a way that I actually leaned back in my seat even though there was ample distance between us, as if the gap had somehow closed in on us.

"Make me your french toast," he said in almost a whisper. "Please."

Me? Luca wanted *me* to cook for *him*?

I could handle a corporate crisis. Could rule a boardroom the way Serena Williams rules a tennis court. I could deal and delegate and dominate with the best CEOs in Manhattan. Luca asking me to cook for him was like Rembrandt asking a kindergartener to paint a portrait. And yet, his tone was so tender that I almost believed I could pull it off.

Without saying a word, I retrieved a loaf of bread that had been baked earlier that morning, four eggs, a stick of butter, and cream—normally I used milk, but changed my mind when I saw the bottle in the refrigerator. Next, I asked Luca for ground cinnamon and vanilla extract, which he produced along with nutmeg, a cast-iron skillet, a mixing bowl, and a long, serrated knife for the bread. I'd never made french toast with fresh Italian bread before.

Setting the bread on the cutting board, I began to saw off six slices.

"Am I holding the knife correctly?" I asked.

He sat still in his seat with the glass of Prosecco, although he didn't touch it. "No lessons," he said. "Just do it the way you want to do it. The way you're used to doing it."

I cracked the eggs, dropped them into the bowl, and beat them with a fork, adding a dash of salt, a considerable amount of cream, and the cinnamon and vanilla, all without the aid of measuring utensils. Even though he'd brought out the nutmeg, I didn't add it. I'd never used it in french toast before. As I beat the mixture, the consistency was almost like custard before setting. Perhaps winging it with the cream was a bad idea. He'd told me to do it the way I was used to doing it. This wasn't it.

I voiced my concerns.

"Don't worry about it," he said. He was so docile; it was equal parts titillating and unnerving.

I went to the stove, ignited the burner, and placed a pat of butter into the skillet—I'd never used cast iron before either—watching it slide around like a figure skater and dissolve into a puddle. Giving the pan a twist to distribute the melted butter, I set up an assembly line: the plate of bread, egg mixture, skillet, and then, on the other side, a clean plate for the finished toast. Timidly I dipped the bread into the egg mixture before fully immersing it, letting the creamy egg and cinnamon envelop it, and then eased it onto the skillet, repeating the step with the next bread slice yet remaining vigilant of the one already nestled in the pan.

"Spatula," I said in a panic, and Luca hopped out of his seat to fetch one for me in the nick of time. I flipped the bread in the skillet to reveal the perfect, golden coat, the vanilla scent pleasurably permeating my senses.

One by one, I settled into a rhythm with the bread slices, dipping and placing and flipping and removing. Using the spatula, I placed half the finished toast on one plate, and then, in an afterthought, attempted to arrange them one overlaying the other asymmetrically instead of side by side or stacked. Presentation really did make a difference, I'd learned. It didn't look artistic, the way I'd seen Luca's presentations, but he seemed delighted by the mere attempt. I made a second attempt with my own plate. When I finished, I turned to find that Luca had set the table for us—including two lit candlesticks.

"Do you have maple syrup?" I asked.

He searched the pantry. "No," he said. "We don't. I'm sorry." After a beat, he said, "I could make a syrup with brown sugar, if you want."

"It's okay," I said, hoping to hide my disappointment. As if the meal had just been ruined. Now I knew why Luca felt the way he did when I picked out the olives.

Luca held up a finger as if to say *I have a solution*, and went to the pantry, returning with a canister of powdered sugar and a sifter, and a bowl of raspberries from the fridge. He spooned some onto each plate, letting them drop with careless abandon onto the toast and roll off onto the plate, and then dusted the sugar, like a snow-topped tree.

"It's pretty," I said. "But not how I used to make it."

"That's okay."

With nervous anticipation, I watched him cut a bite-sized triangle from one of the slices and place it into his mouth, closing his eyes as he did. God, even his lashes were gorgeous. Long and thick.

He's going to hate it. Going to think, "What did I expect from the queen of processed pasta, the microwave monster?" He'll be nice and not insult me this time, but he'll spit it out when I'm not looking.

He finished chewing and opened his eyes. I couldn't even bring myself to say, "Well?" although I was on the edge of my seat, stiffened by the suspense.

Luca met my eyes with those black, obsidian pools of his, framed by the silky strands of his bangs and sharp cheekbones, and his entire expression softened and warmed. I could actually see it morph. He looked youthful. He glowed. He looked . . . *full*.

"This is the best french toast I've ever tasted, Miss Katie. Thank you."

My heart expanded with every beat, like it was going to break through my breastbone.

"That's very kind of you to say, Luca. But I'm sure a man with your palate and expertise and world experience has tasted way better. I mean, sure, it's not made with Wonder Bread this time, but—"

Luca leaned over and brought his berry-scented fingers to my lips to keep them from moving. My entire body tingled and goose bumps appeared on my arms.

"You don't understand," he said, again in a whispery breath. "I hope someday you will."

We ate the rest of our french toast in a strangely comfortable silence (and I have to say, it *was* the best I'd ever made, even without the maple syrup) and polished off the bottle of Prosecco. Which, in hindsight, was probably what prompted me to invite Luca to dance the tango with me, and what prompted him to oblige. I'd taught Max the dance—we were planning to do it at our wedding reception—but Luca already knew it. Of course. With every step and turn and pull, the heat between us intensified. And it was probably the Prosecco and the heat and Luca's sturdy hands and firm body and the vanilla and cinnamon and raspberry scents that somehow wafted us to the couch in the parlor after he dipped me and then held me there as he planted a long, sultry kiss on my powdered sugar-coated lips.

Him, sitting upright. Me, straddling him. Us, removing each other's shirts like they were banana peels, running our hands all over our bare chests and torsos, kissing, smelling, tasting each other's skin. He rose from the chair, lifting me with him, seeming to pause only for a second, as if to test my weight. My legs coiled around him, clutching for dear life, as he carried me upstairs to his bedroom.

This. This was why I killed myself at the gym and measured every carrot stick and deprived myself of bagels and cheesecake.

He set me down in the room lit only by moonbeams, closed the door and locked it, and then took hold and fervently kissed me again, peeling off yet another layer of clothing, lowering me on the bed. He cupped my breasts and ran his thumb along them the way I saw him test a tomato for ripeness. Let down my ponytail and untangled my hair as delicately and playfully as he untangled fresh fettuccine noodles. Licked each of my fingers like frosting on a spoon. Meanwhile, I kneaded his shoulders the way he kneaded dough. Inhaled him as if I were inhaling the scent of newly baked bread, or melted chocolate, or simmering, bubbling sauce.

Luca was delicious. Delectable. Heavenly.

And just as he latched his fingers onto my lace bikini briefs, about to peel away the final layer, we locked into a gaze. I recognized the look in his eyes, and it consumed me with all the warmth of an apple pie.

I broke into a satisfied smile. "You look at me the way you look at food," I murmured.

And then I watched his eyes digest this piece of information, and turn from delight to bewilderment in an instant.

"Pretend I'm a Reese's," I said with a giggle, and kissed him again, ready for us to devour each other in pure, sweet, sexual splendor.

Luca paused, and then leapt up from the bed in revulsion.

"No, Miss Katie."

I hoisted myself up and felt woozy, as if someone had just beaned me with a frying pan.

"Wh—what?"

"This is not going to happen," he said, his voice cold and flat.

"What, because I teased you about the peanut butter cup? Look, I'm—"

He snapped on the light, blinding us both, recouped his pants from the floor and shot them up his legs. "It's not that. Clearly there are many reasons why this is a bad idea."

Suddenly feeling exposed, I covered my breasts with my hands and retrieved my pajama bottoms from the floor— we'd left our tops downstairs.

"Name them, please," I said.

Luca yanked a T-shirt from his duffel bag and tossed it to me.

"You yourself said yesterday that we're business partners. I've slept with women I've worked with before. It never ends well, and it always winds up costing me money. That's one. Two is that you live in New York and I live here, and we are both extremely busy, so let's not even pretend that this would go beyond tonight."

He didn't even take a breath for me to get a word in. "Third . . . " he started, and paused as if trying to think of a reason, ". . . you're not my type."

I raised a hand to halt him. "*Whoa*," I said, seething. "What did you just say?"

"You're too skinny. Never have I carried a woman up the stairs. Or over a threshold. I prefer women who are more . . . fleshy. It felt like I was going to snap you like a twig."

Seriously? *SERIOUSLY????*

"So, your nibbling my earlobe just now . . . that's you totally turned off."

"That was the Prosecco," he replied.

No. I was not going to be humiliated like this again. Screw that-was-the-Prosecco. Screw Butterfinger wrappers on the floor. Screw these men with their rationalizations and their rejections and their refusal to let me in.

"You are such a liar, Luca," I said, enunciating every word venomously. "Not only that, but you're a really bad one."

"If it makes you feel better about yourself to think that, then fine. I can live with it."

I exploded. "You *asshole!* You *know* something happened between us just now. And whatever it is that freaked you out, you're trying to blame me! Well, that is *not* going to happen. I spent months blaming myself for my fiancé betraying my love and trust by taking another woman to my bed—*my* bed—and lying about it. And here you are lying through your teeth to me, hurting me in the worst way possible, all because . . . whatever, I don't even know. Well, *screw you, Caramelli!*"

I brushed past him and stormed down to my bedroom, shaking so bad that my rib cage felt ready to cave in on my heart. *Not again, not again, please, not again . . . There wasn't even any coconut this time.*

What had I done wrong? Was it the french toast? Was it something I said?

Was it *me*?

No. It wasn't me. Not this time. *Please, no.*

Just as I was about to slam the door, Luca appeared in front of me, looking forlorn.

"You feed me, Katie," he said quietly. "That's the reason."

I slammed the door on him.

And then, when the anger subsided just enough for me to think, I heard the words. *You feed me.* And when I opened the door and charged down the hall to ask him to explain them to me, Gianluca Caramelli was gone.

nineteen

I swear I had whiplash from how it all came to a grinding halt, and then crashed and burned.

Luca was gone. No good-bye, no explanation, nothing. Didn't even tell his sister he was taking off. Didn't matter, because we were contractually stuck with each other now.

Not only that, but I had a headache the following morning from the Prosecco. Shit-fritters.

At least with Max there had been a reason—he cheated on me. End of story. And I got to kick him out before he left. (And would he have eventually left? Just how long would he have carried on with Cheetah? I hated that that thought still kept me awake some nights.) But last night had left me clueless. Sure, Luca had given me reasons, but not a single one of them rang true except *You feed me*, and I still needed elaboration on that one. There was no way I could have imagined that our attraction was mutual. Even less likely was that it was all a Prosecco-induced spell that Luca had somehow broken free of right before he was about to enter me. No matter how many times I replayed the scene in my head, I couldn't figure out what went wrong, what I'd said that could have made him stop when he was sporting a hard-on and leave me there to put out my own fire and tend to the wound left from all the stabs he took at my heart.

Too skinny? Not his type? I would cost him money?

Idiot.

But he was trying to tell me something. *You feed me.* What, just because I made him french toast? It wasn't *that* good. Plus, he asked me to. And it's not like I held the fork for him. It had to *mean something*. It seemed all I'd done the entire week was feed his disgust.

I slammed the door in his face. I told him to screw himself.

He deserved it.

He'd also said his grandfather would have liked me. Hadn't he held his grandfather's word in high regard? Or maybe he'd changed his mind. Maybe the ghost of his grandfather had whispered to Luca, *Surely you can do better than her.* Strange timing, but that would've freaked me out.

My pajama top had mysteriously materialized on the chest of drawers, neatly folded, when I awoke. It must have been Luciana, who didn't need a detective to figure out how and/ or why it had ended up on the parlor floor. Her new business partner banged her brother. Or so she thought. Probably thought I slept with my entire board of directors too.

I couldn't wait to get out of the villa. Out of Genoa and away from all traces of Gianluca Caramelli. To go back to my company and my house and my Pasta Pronto meals patiently waiting in my fridge. Back to my gym schedule so I could burn off the gazillion pounds I'd put on since I arrived, if not more—I hadn't weighed myself since the morning I left New York. Heck, my thighs were starting to take the shape of biscotti.

About to zip my suitcase closed, I spied Luca's sacrificial T-shirt on the chair in the corner. I'd pulled it off like it was germ-infested and chucked it there after I discovered Luca had left last night.

Don't smell it, don't smell it, don't smell it . . .

I picked it up and inhaled Luca Caramelli one last time. But at least I defeated the temptation to add it to my suitcase and abandoned it on the chair when I exited the room and closed the door behind me.

Luciana greeted me in the kitchen with a spread of biscotti and berries and fresh whipped cream and espresso. I was going to miss this.

She was a friendlier form of her brother. Not just in looks, but also in presence, as if she'd never had a troublesome day in her life. And if she had, it was nothing a little hospitality couldn't cure. Even without makeup, her skin glowed, with apple cheeks and cherry lips and olive skin and silky hair. And yet, she was also a savvy businesswoman, demonstrated by her demeanor when we sat down with the lawyers to sign the papers.

I could barely face her. Could feel my cheeks flush with embarrassment, as if she'd seen more than my pajama top on the floor.

"Luciana, I—" I started.

She interrupted me. "—Luca has disappeared on us once again. Back to Alba, I assume. I apologize for his rudeness."

"Did he . . . did he say anything?"

"I didn't even see him leave."

I glanced at her for only one second, desperate to confess everything to her, to persuade her that never in my life had I behaved so unprofessionally, that I hadn't been myself since catching my fiancé in a Butterfinger-wrapper-littered bed with a hostess, that if she wanted to nullify the contract, I would understand and even pay all the legal fees. All I saw were kind, compassionate, forgiving eyes looking back at me.

She knew. She knew something wasn't right.

She held out a plate. "Have something to eat, Katie."

And then I lost it. Just stood there in front of her, my face crumpled up, tears leaking out and dripping from my chin, the full-out ugly cry.

Luciana poured a glass of wine and handed it to me with a cloth napkin.

"I didn't mean to," I cried. "It just happened. Or rather, it almost happened. It was going to happen, and then it didn't, and then . . . I know it shouldn't have in the first place."

"Whatever happened, Katie, I know my brother well enough to know it probably wasn't your fault. He behaved badly. Anyone who walks out behaves badly. I feel partly responsible. I should have kept a better eye on him. And I should have warned you. But given the way you two clashed that first day, I didn't think . . ."

"I've never done this before," I said, my eyes trained to the floor in shame. "Ever. Especially with someone I'm in business with."

"I believe you," she said. "But Katie, I'm not pleased. This is a difficult beginning to our partnership." She planted her hands on my shoulders to steady me. "Today you go to the airport and fly back to New York. Forget Luca. He wanted nothing to do with any of this anyway, right? Let him go back to Alba and his trattoria. You and I will work without him."

She was no-nonsense. I needed that in a business partner. But it wasn't what I *wanted*. I wanted her to be kind. Encouraging. A friend.

I hadn't had a friend in so long. I hadn't *been* a friend in so long.

And I desperately wanted one, and to be one, more than anything in the world.

twenty
Two weeks later

'd returned to my house in Dix Hills to find everything as I'd left it. I'd hired a neighbor who was a grad student to house-sit. (Always ask a grad student—they're way too stressed out and anal to party, until their thesis is done. Then they get wrecked.)

And yet, everything *felt* different. The furniture looked as if it had been staged rather than purchased by me. The wall art looked lifeless. The place was plant-less. And after poring over the ubiquitous Caramelli family photos in the villa, the absence of family photos—of *any* photos—in my home was conspicuous. The rolling hills and vineyard rows and industrial structures of Alba and Genoa had been replaced by curbside fire hydrants and mailboxes and streetlamps.

Not only that, but my clothes were tight. Like, *really* tight. I think even my toes had expanded.

I'd absorbed quite a bit of knowledge after watching Luca and Alberto and the entire staff at Trattoria Naturale at work. By the time I left, I'd sampled just about everything on the menu.

I missed Luca terribly. Missed his delectable scent. And let's not even mention how much I was missing siesta. I nearly snored during a meeting with one of the VPs the other day.

Something else had changed upon my return that I found even more disturbing than the fact that I could barely zip up and button my skirts—and you'd think that would've been the end of the world for me; three weeks ago it most certainly would have been. On my first full day back from Italy, while getting over the jet lag, I settled for my Pasta Pronto meals rather than go to the store to buy groceries. One: The fact that I used the word "settled" was the first sign of change. I'd *never* considered eating my product "settling." Going out to dinner was "settling." Making cinnamon toast for dinner was "settling." Two: After removing the plastic covering, I noticed for the first time how cold and stiff and lifeless the pasta looked on the microwavable cardboard plate. It looked . . . unappealing.

And then I tasted it.

My favorite Pasta Pronto meal had always been the fettuccine alfredo. Creamy and comforting and perfectly portioned. Steam a little broccoli and I could add the green not only to my plate but also my color chart, thus making my skinny avatar smile.

One bite and I nearly gagged. I didn't dare attempt a second bite.

Maybe it was the jet lag, I told myself. Or, God forbid, another defective product.

So I took out the Pasta Puttanesca ("Puttanesca the fun in your mouth and not on your hips!" said the box), nuked it, and tasted.

Crap.

The Three-Cheese-is-a Charm Tortellini: crap.

The Low-Carb Carbonara: crap.

The Manicotti of Your Dreams: crappity crap crap.

Every single one of them tasted like cellophane and salt.

Holy frappe, had Gianluca been right all this time? Had all my critics? Had I been making nothing but microwaved chemical composites? Had I duped millions of women into thinking they were eating something delicious and healthy?

And if the answer was yes, then what did that mean for my company? What did it mean for the future of Pasta Pronto, and for the "A Taste of Genoa" meals that Luci and I had begun to envision? My mission statement? My life's work? What did it mean for *me*?

The public relations team meeting began promptly at nine o'clock Monday morning. I arranged for biscotti and fruit to be delivered to the boardroom from the company cafeteria. Yeah. Still nothing like Luca's.

"So we've come up with the *perfect* event to promote your new product line with the Caramellis," said Wendy Blount with an enthusiasm you saw in most car salespeople. "It'll make Pasta Pronto a household name again—and in a good way—and it'll drum up excitement for the new collaboration."

"Let's hear it," I said.

The team fired up their PowerPoint presentation. On the first slide, in flashy red type, blazed the words PASTA WARS!

"A one-night-only competition show on the Flavor Channel. Think *Throwdown with Bobby Flay* meets *Iron Chef*. An epic battle of pasta royalty," said Wendy.

"Who battles whom?" I asked.

Wendy's assistant clicked to the next slide, and side-by-side press photos of me and Gianluca, respectively, filled the projector screen. I practically recoiled in my chair as knots twisted in my stomach.

"The Pasta Pronto Queen versus the Caramelli King! You said you learned how to make fresh pasta, didn't you? Well, this will shut all Pasta Pronto's critics up once and for all."

"Won't that undermine our product and our mission?" I asked.

"It'll shut Gianluca Caramelli up!" Wendy said, completely ignoring the question.

"Not if he wins," I said.

"That's what will make it so epic! Who wins—you or him? Everyone will be on the edge of their seats!" Wendy said everything like a fifteen-year-old getting psyched for a boy band concert.

"You can't be serious, Wendy. I made only two batches of pasta. And they were terrible. In fact, the second batch resulted in me burning my foot when I spilled boiling water on it. Luca—*Gianluca*—has been making it since he was a kid. There's no competition."

"Not if you *train*, Katie! And we'll make that part of the show—film clips of you meeting with the leading pasta experts in New York, practicing in a test kitchen. . . . It'll be *fab*ulous. Gianluca won't expect it!"

It would be kind of fun to surprise him. Show him that I could actually make halfway decent pasta without burning any limbs. And who knows? Maybe I *could* beat him. Especially if he thought he didn't have to try. Like the tortoise and the hare. I could be a fiercely competitive tortoise when I wanted to be.

And suddenly I wanted to beat Luca. Big time.

"There's no way he would get on board with something like this," I said. "He detests celebrity chefs and reality cooking shows and all that."

"Do you know how many public appearances he's made over the years?" asked Wendy's assistant. "Maybe not as many in the States, but he's a big deal in Europe. Trust me, this guy is not camera shy. And his agent already said he's on board."

I nearly choked on the strawberry I'd just bit into. "*He's on board???* And he has *an agent*??? Since when?"

"Since we called him last week. His agent responded in twenty-four hours."

I was completely flummoxed. "You called *him* before you called *me?*"

"We were going to pitch it to you while you were still in Italy, but then you informed us of your return, and we figured you'd need a few days to get back up to speed. . . ."

I considered inquiring who on my scheduling staff approved of this postponement, but the damage was already done.

I sighed and wearily rubbed my eyes. "When would this happen?"

"The competition will happen in exactly sixty days," said Wendy. "The show will air three months after that. We've already sold ad space for Pasta Pronto for those three months leading up to the premiere."

My head spun—*sixty days*? How was I supposed to match Luca's expertise in sixty days? How could they have booked this thing without approaching me first? And why on earth did Mr. I-Refuse-to-be-a-Sellout agree to do a mainstream competition show—in the States, no less—with *me*, the woman he rejected? Would we have to see each other beforehand? Would we do joint press events?

Which then brought me to thoughts of seeing Luca. The mental image of his lips suckling my nipples one minute and announcing *This isn't happening* the next and then disappearing altogether blurred my vision of the PowerPoint screen.

Oh yeah. I was gonna crush him.

"Let's go to war," I said.

twenty~one

I was gaining weight. I was definitely gaining weight. My clothes told me so. My mirror told me so. And I'd be lying if I said it didn't concern me. However, since my return from Genoa, everyone who knew me complimented how "healthy" I looked. At first I thought it was some kind of condescending equivalent of "nice going, fatty," but the expressions on their faces told me something different. It was as if people were breathing a sigh of relief.

"Geez, you'd think I'd been starving myself all these months the way everyone is acting," I said to Jennifer, my assistant.

"It's not that," she replied. "It's just that you've always been, well . . . *preoccupied* with your body image."

She practically cowered upon catching herself and apologized profusely, as if I was about to fire her on the spot for crossing a professional line. I saw it neither as overstepping a boundary nor as a criticism, however. The words were a splash of cold water, biting and awakening and flinch-inducing. *Vigilant* was the descriptor I'd always used. But even that suddenly spoke of paranoia, fixation, like constantly checking a door with ten deadbolts just to make sure it's locked.

"I appreciate your being so straightforward," I said. "Really. I had no idea it was that obvious."

"There's nothing wrong with wanting to be a healthy weight," she added. "It's why you started Pasta Pronto—to give women an opportunity to be that without having to deprive themselves. But you've exchanged one deprivation for another."

If I didn't know better, I'd have sworn she was channeling Luca Caramelli at that moment.

Even my skin tone had changed, looking more luminous and less washed out.

A new daily routine developed in the coming weeks:

5:00 AM: Bike ride, and not a stationary one (I never did care for yoga).

6:00 AM: Shower and light breakfast—no more skipping meals.

7:00 AM: Commute to Manhattan via car service.

9:00 AM–1:00 PM: Work.

1:00 PM: Lunch. In the past, when I didn't allot my lunch hour to a business meeting, I either ate a salad or a Pasta Pronto meal at my desk or skipped it altogether. Now I would request the cooks in the HQ cafeteria (which, of course, kept a hefty supply of Pasta Pronto meals), to fix me a hearty antipasto plate and some form of protein, like grilled chicken. Sometimes I even went to the kitchen and did it myself. On days I dined at a restaurant, rather than logging color codes and calories, instead I logged my order, why I ordered it, and feedback on what I liked or didn't like about it. Continuing the Italian practice of reversing lunch and dinner in terms of meal size and attention produced positive effects on my energy.

Moreover, I was learning about food in a way I'd never approached it before—*personal*. One-on-one. Not a matter of convenience, but consciousness. Not a matter of business, but relationship. I was learning what I liked and didn't like about certain foods and how they made me feel. I was learning what my body liked and didn't like. And I hadn't counted a single calorie or color-charted even a grape.

3:00 PM: Siesta. Or, at least, my version of it. No calls, no appointments, nothing for the entire hour. The first half consisted of a power nap on the couch in my office. The second half resulted in a jaunt around the building in which I stopped and chatted with employees, asked them what they were working on, et cetera. I felt more connected to my company than I had in years. All those years of spouting team-oriented platitudes, and I was finally acting like a team player rather than a control freak. I wasn't sure if that was the result of my time spent in close contact with the staff at Trattoria Naturale or my partnering with Luciana. Maybe both. Or neither.

4:00 PM: resume work agenda.

5:30 PM: Return commute to Dix Hills.

7:00—9:00 PM: Practice making pasta for the *Pasta Wars* competition. I'd come home from Genoa to find a brand-new pasta maker waiting for me—a gift from Luciana to celebrate our new partnership—and had used it every night since the press release about the competition. Usually I packed whatever I made and either gave it to my grad student neighbor or took it to work the next day for my staff, unless I really fouled up a recipe. I was getting very good at linguini shrimp scampi. I still needed to work on not over-stuffing the ravioli. I hadn't yet gotten daring with pasta shapes like tortellini and rotini and gnocchi.

During this time block I also made a light supper, like the kinds I had in Italy, usually soup or salad or a small piece of fish. I even made french toast one night, despite every bite making me long for the sight of Luca, as well as his voice and scent and taste and touch.

I hadn't eaten a single Pasta Pronto meal since that last day I'd sampled them all and found them—dare I say it—abominable. Couldn't even look at them.

9:00 PM: Go over daily receipts for Trattoria Naturale and check in with Alberto via email. With Luci's help, I outlined a new budget and told Alberto he had to be assertive with Luca in terms of enforcing it. So far the firm hand was working, and Luca was keeping his spending at bay.

10:00 PM: Bedtime. I used to stay up until twelve, one in the morning with work. But I couldn't even keep my eyes open anymore, and I'd given up the nighttime caffeine. And yet, despite losing those extra hours, I was more productive and ahead of my work than ever. The never-ending influx of emails didn't overwhelm me as much. The petty executive squabbles didn't peck at me. And I had more pep after one bike ride than I did following the one hundred sit-ups and all the other back-breaking, sweat-inducing exercises I used to pound out. Each day I was edging closer to balancing the pressures of corporate demands with personal pleasures.

Maybe a simple life wasn't the key after all. Maybe *balance* was. And maybe that's what Luca was aiming for.

Now if only I could get over my sexual frustration. . . .

twenty~two

The *Pasta Wars* press event was a smashing success, especially on social media. Wendy's team set up a drawing to win Pasta Pronto product giveaways, free tickets to the taping of the competition, and the grand prize: a trip to Caramelli's restaurant in Genoa. #TeamCravens and #TeamCaramelli instantly flooded Twitter. Pasta Pronto sales saw an immediate uptick, and Caramelli's restaurant also reaped the benefits.

The press conference Q and A, however, was another story. According to Wendy, Luca had refused to do a satellite hookup, but the PR team told the media that he was ill the morning of the event. Honestly, I was relieved not to see those piercing eyes and long lashes and inky hair.

The first couple of questions were harmless, nothing I hadn't fielded before.

Q: Ms. Cravens, do you really think you have a chance to beat Chef Caramelli?

ME: Well, given that I spent a week in Italy watching the master Caramelli at work, I'd say I picked up a secret or two.

Q: How do you respond to Chef Caramelli's public dismissals of your Pasta Pronto meals?

ME: I think our customers have already responded by continuing to make our pasta meals part of their daily lifestyles.

Q: What do you consider to be your pasta specialty?

ME: I don't know if I have one yet.

Then this happened:

Q: Ms. Cravens, I have a quote from Chef Caramelli saying: "Katie Cravens doesn't even know how to boil water without needing medical attention." What do you have to say to him in response?

You know how in TV shows or movies when the shutter-clicks and the microphones and the geeselike chatter goes silent the moment *the* question is asked? That's what it felt like—as if all activity froze. As if time itself froze. My still-recovering foot tingled with anger and humiliation. I could almost hear Luca's smarmy tone, see his dismissive hand and his emphatic eye rolls.

Fuming, I clutched the sides of the podium, wishing instead I could clutch Luca's throat. So *this* was why he got on board? So he could insult me and flaunt my most vulnerable moments? It wasn't enough to reject me sexually?

I swallowed hard, my mouth suddenly dry and pasty. "No comment."

Q: What was the most important lesson you learned in Italy?

Don't trust douchebags who treat your heart like it's a piece of veal.

Me: I learned the proper way to use a kitchen knife.

Q: What do you consider to be Chef Caramelli's specialty?

My head was swimming. My eyes were twitching. My foot was throbbing. My heart was hurting.

The innuendo, although not intentional, poked me on the shoulder.

"I didn't really get the chance to find out," I said with a bite of sarcasm.

And then the hinges came off. "Is Gianluca Caramelli a great chef? Yes. But he's also a condescending, self-absorbed jerk who's incapable of any sort of change. And that's why I will win this pasta war. Because *I* adapt. What do I have to say to him? You tell Luca that at least I don't turn off the burner just because it's too hot. You tell him that *I* don't run and hide from a fight. You tell him . . . tell him I'm going to *beat* him in this pasta war."

And with that the strobe lights flashed and the shutters clicked and the reporters buzzed and I turned to find Wendy looking like the public relations cat who just ate the canary. A gorgeous, Italian hunk of a canary. And I was the one who fed it to her.

twenty~three

I left the podium shell-shocked while an oblivious Wendy spouted out praise in rapid-fire speed. "That was *fab*-u-lous, Katie! You just turned this thing into an *event*! The food blogs are going to pick it up. It's trending on Twitter. We may even be able to get Ted Allen to MC it instead of that teen idol hack."

"What teen idol hack?"

"Toby-someone."

How could I have said all those things? In public? On the record? I called Luca Caramelli a condescending, self-absorbed jerk. Ohmigod, I called him *Luca*—now everyone knew we'd become something more than professional. Geez, why didn't I just tell them about the tango in the parlor and the carrying up the stairs and the nakedness and the . . .

Hang on. He started it.

I mean, where did he get off making that crack about the boiling water and my foot injury? What kind of coward says such a thing about someone he rejects and then deserts in the middle of the night and doesn't even have the scones to show up for a press event he got on board for?

No. Luca got what he deserved. And it wasn't like I said anything untrue.

But Luciana wouldn't appreciate it. Luca was her twin brother. Her first and best friend in the world. She knew his flaws, but it didn't mean she didn't love him.

There was still enough time before the day was over in Genoa for me to call her.

Luci answered the phone and I recounted the press conference Q and A. After a pregnant pause, she said, "That doesn't sound at all like my brother."

"What do you mean?" I asked.

"He can be rude, but he's not mean. That was mean."

"Oh, and 'microwave bastardization' wasn't mean? He said those things too."

"But he didn't know you then. He knows you now. And although he might still disagree with you, I don't think he would say such things publicly, especially since he signed our contracts and agreed to do this competition to promote the new pasta line."

It wasn't that I expected her to take my side over his, or that I expected her to take any side at all. And yet, her defense of Luca still irked me.

"I'm still shocked he agreed to do the show, given how he constantly rails against celebrity chefs and all that," I said.

"My brother says a lot of things contrary to what he really thinks," said Luci.

Did he not really mean all those things he said when he rejected me? Or maybe he didn't really mean *You feed me*.

"When I speak to him I'll tell him you feel badly about what you said in response," she said before adding, "but it's time to get back to work, Katie."

"I am back to work."

"Your statements at the press conference say otherwise. Whatever happened here between you and Luca, it's done."

Like I didn't already know that.

"I'm a professional, but I'm also human," I said. "Cut me some slack."

"You assured me that you don't mix business with your personal life. I'm just trying to maintain that boundary for the sake of the success of this partnership."

"You have nothing to worry about, Luciana," I said, my tone gone cold. "And now if you'll excuse me, I need to get back to work."

What stung more than anything else was that she was right. It *was* time to get back to work. Back to developing the new pasta line, back to running the company, back to practicing my pasta-making technique, and while I was at it, maybe it was time to get back on my old regimen and dump this new routine. This was New York, not Alba or Genoa. A cutthroat city demanded a cutthroat routine. Time to get my head out of the kitchen—specifically, Luca's kitchen—and back into the game.

After some Prosecco, I decided.

As congratulations for a well-executed promotion and press event (Q and A not withstanding), I took Wendy and her PR team out for drinks after work. Strictly business, I rationalized.

Except I might have had one too many glasses of Prosecco. Or maybe three too many.

"You did *great*," said a rather buzzed Wendy. "People *love* this stuff. By the time the show tapes you'll have everyone rooting for you. That's what you want. Don't worry about Gianluca. He's a big boy. And he can certainly dish it out."

"But, if it's a partnership . . ." I started, leaning in to Wendy and bumping heads with her by accident. We both giggled.

"It's *business*. The Caramellis are a brand name as much as they're a family. They know what's what."

"I know that," I said. "Precisely why I shouldn't have spoken out about a business associate."

"Gianluca has said plenty about you."

"Before we got into bed with each other," I pointed out. Wendy's eyes widened, and I quickly backpedaled. "It's *a figure of speech*!" We both broke into another round of giggling.

I stumbled out to the car that had arranged to meet me where we had drinks. Once inside, I closed my eyes and, seemingly seconds later, opened them in my driveway, where the driver was calling my name and informing me that we were home. Inside the cavernous house, I broke the silence by sarcastically calling out for Max and laughing afterward as I kicked off my pumps. Screw fart-cheering Max and his dirty socks.

My body felt ready to burst out of my clothes like the Incredible Hulk, my suit clinging to the flesh rolls beginning to fold over my belly and waistline. The skirt was the first to go, followed by the jacket and blouse and bra and even bikini briefs.

Katie Cravens, in the flesh.

And getting fleshier by the minute.

Would Luca like *this* body? I wondered.

And no sooner than I wondered did my body feel all warm and tingly and yearn to be touched.

Strutting to my bed (although I was soused, so realistically it was probably more of a staggering sway), I picked up my phone and texted Luca:

I'm naked right now. Completely, totally naked. And horny. Plus I smell like vanilla. And I'm so heavy now you probably couldn't even carry me five steps. So just live with that image in your head. I'm everything you wanted. Right here, right now

I followed up with one more text before getting in bed and pulling up the covers:

Douche move, Caramelli

twenty~four

Is there a word to describe waking up and instantly knowing you've done something stupid without remembering it? Because that's exactly what happened the moment I opened my eyes and the Prosecco-pounding drum reverberated against my temples. Not to mention I was naked.

Ugh.

The phone was involved. That much I knew. I perused the call log. Nothing. Then I opened text messages.

Oh. God.

I didn't.

But I did.

The drunk text.

I hadn't even drunk-texted Max following our breakup. Maybe because once he cheated on me, he pretty much felt dead to me. That is, until I found out he and Cheetah were engaged. But even then I'd managed self-control.

Well, unless you call attempting to make pasta in the middle of the night and spilling boiling water on my foot "self-control."

With the time difference, Luca would have received the text in the peak of evening, while he was wide awake and at Trattoria Naturale, where he probably showed it to Alberto and the staff.

And sonofabitch, the stupid autocorrect changed Luca's last name to "Caramello." Because sending a drunk text informing Luca that I was naked and horny for him wasn't mortifying enough. I had to be illiterate as well. *Douche move, Caramello.* Brilliant.

At least I'd had the good sense not to snap and send a photo. Even drunk I knew the disastrous repercussions of that. Besides, I'd wanted Luca to get the full effect of what he was missing—my memory had recovered that detail.

But I repeat: *ugh.*

Had Luca ever sent a drunk text to anyone? I suddenly wondered. Had he ever experienced a moment of lost inhibition, where alcohol vanquished vulnerability and made him opt for the easy, comfortable, and safe bet? Or had he been closed off for so long that he'd never gotten to that level where he missed someone enough to forfeit dignity?

Thing is, the absence of vulnerability was a smoke screen—the drunk text was hardcore proof of just how vulnerable and insecure and frightened you really were.

And now, Luca knew. He had the upper hand. And he was surely going to use it against me, especially once he found out about what I said during the press conference.

Would he be low enough to share the drunk text with the media?

No. That would damage *his* credibility and reputation as much as it would mine. Plus it would give up any leverage he'd have against me. No, he was going to use psychological warfare to win the *Pasta Wars* competition. As if his talent didn't already make him a shoo-in.

Worst of all, I couldn't fix this. I had to leave the text out there. To text him again and tell him to disregard it would only give him more power. And I had no intention of speaking to him in person, not until the competition, when it would be mandatory. No, I had to sit there and do nothing, and be the fool Luca Caramelli now knew me to be.

twenty-five

With just weeks to go before the taping of *Pasta Wars*, I did a promotional segment of getting a "cooking lesson" from my "pasta coach," Cass Brophy, the punky, sassy chef on the Flavor Channel. Her show, *Spaghetti Pie*, was born the moment she won *Chopped* by wowing the judges with a baked concoction of spaghetti, peaches, and a molasses-based glaze as the dessert course. Standing five foot two with flaming red hair like those troll dolls you played with as a kid, pixied and spiked on top, she was well-schooled in Italian cuisine even though she was a native Montanan. Said in an interview: "There's nothing interesting or cultural about Montana cuisine except for Rocky Mountain oysters—one bite of those and you want to migrate east." A quick Google search revealed Rocky Mountain oysters to be, in actuality, cow's balls.

Shooting the segment took most of the day. It was actually quite fun, meeting Chef Cass and being fawned over like a star and goofing around in front of the cameras once my self-consciousness wore off. After the segment, Chef Cass complimented my pasta-making skills even though I was still clearly an amateur. I had no idea what kind of pasta Luca and I would be challenged to make—we weren't going to find out until an hour before the competition started—but Chef Cass said it would probably be something like a ravioli or a tortellini along with a dish where making the actual pasta was easy but the sauce would be a challenge. In other words, "Americanized," as Luca would say.

"Your pasta-making technique is good," Chef Cass said on camera, dressed in her familiar wardrobe of painted-splattered T-shirts and geometrical patterned skirts, ripped jeans cuffed at the ankles, and neon Doc Martens—a throwback to the renowned FLIP clothing store in New York during the eighties. "Now get to work on learning some sauces." She recommended a few, and after the shoot I asked Luciana to send me some recipes as well as a way to smooth things over from our last conversation and assist in the development of our pasta line.

Chef Cass and I hit it off so well that the following week she invited me to her restaurant and gave me a tour. There she taught me how to make gnocchi; mine were spectacular failures, while hers caused us to both do a little happy dance. She also invited me to shoot an episode of *Spaghetti Pie* with her that would air after *Pasta Wars*, when viewers would be more likely to recognize me. She "recreated" Pasta Pronto's three best sellers and taught me how to make them myself (with the caveat that the calorie counts were nowhere near the vicinity of the Pasta Pronto meals). Cass was also diplomatic in not bashing Pasta Pronto or frozen food, and instead offered the pros and cons of both versions.

Despite my enjoyment of watching Luca cook, he never made it feel pleasurable when *I* tried to do it. Cass, on the other hand, made it fun. She excused mistakes. She encouraged me at every turn.

Maybe that's what cooking with a friend was supposed to be.

It had been so long since I laughed, since I'd spent late-night hours talking to someone, letting down my guard, sharing secrets. Within no time Cass had become someone with which to do just that. What's more, in addition to being a world-class chef and Flavor Channel celebrity, she had a good head for business. She was someone I trusted. Thus, when she asked, "Have you and Luciana considered making a fresh line of pasta rather than frozen? Because you could totally pull it off. And I think it would broaden your customer base as well as win you some points with your naysayers," I seriously considered it.

"You're a great person, Katie," she said. "I think who you are and what you sell don't match up."

Was that a backhanded compliment, or was she trying to tell me something increasingly difficult to deny? It reminded me of when Luca alluded to my blonde hair being "fake," not to mention the scandalous secret I was still hiding: that my own product line had become completely inedible to me.

What had I been trying to sell all these years?

A way to have it all. A way to be in control.

Control. Wasn't that what it always came back to?

For years my mother had controlled what we did and didn't eat. She controlled the fate of her marriage by withholding one of two things: food or sex. Both, actually.

I controlled what I wanted the world to see: Katie Cravens, entrepreneur. Katie Cravens, thin person with fit body. Katie Cravens, wealthy, successful, has-it-all, including wealthy, successful, handsome husband. Or so I thought. Katie Cravens, unwilling to give an inch, especially where her waistline was concerned.

Who you are and what you sell don't match up.

If that was true, then who was I really? Was I not successful? Did I not have it all? I mean, obviously the husband thing didn't work out.

Was I not in control?

If who I was had been a lie all this time, then who did I want to be? What did I want to sell?

The next day, I made an appointment to dye my hair back to its natural brunette shade. With some caramel highlights for the hell of it. When I sent Cass a selfie, she replied:

I feel like I've finally seen the real Katie. And she's as lovely as can be

———

Days before the competition, Stu Chutney, the president of Happy Brands, Inc., invited me to lunch. I made the appointment, hung up the phone, inhaled and exhaled a freak-out breath, and said to no one, "Holy shit, he wants to buy the company."

Of course Stu said nothing of the kind over the phone, didn't even hint at it, but I *knew*. Why else would he call out of the blue? I immediately summoned my legal team. "Get me everything you can on Happy Brands. I think Stu Chutney wants to make a move on Pasta Pronto." I knew the company owned an array of household brands ranging from cleaners to condiments to candy. A diet pasta line would be a nice addition to their repertoire, I guessed.

Stu was the business equivalent of a "frenemy." We met at Cass's restaurant, Franca Fortunado (I wanted the upper hand of being on familiar turf), and I recommended the gnocchi in basil pesto to Stu while I ordered seared prosciutto and pineapple crostini sprinkled with lemon juice. No alcohol—I wanted to keep my wits about me.

Once Gisela, our server, took our orders and departed, I folded my cloth napkin over my lap and Stu smiled at me.

"You're looking well, Katie. I heard all about this televised pasta competition you're doing. Sounds like fun."

"It's been great PR," I said.

Stu smiled, showing off straight, white, capped shark teeth. "Well, that's just great. Business should be fun, don't you think?"

"Cut the crap, Stu," I said after swallowing a sip of water from a wine glass. "Your stock is underperforming. Your cash cows are stagnant. Your loss leaders aren't leading anymore. Your last launch fizzled. And you've got a stockholder's meeting coming up. You'd love to give them some good news, wouldn't you?"

Stu looked at me, seemingly impressed. It never failed—the boys were always surprised when the girls could play their game. He made a *You found me out* gesture.

"I've been watching Pasta Pronto for a while, Katie," he said. "Even before the health scare—which you handled very well, by the way. Business schools should adopt it as a case study of what to do. You recovered well. But recently you seem to have lost . . . focus."

Good lord, did it really show?

"How so?" I asked, not batting an eye. I had an excellent poker face when it came to business. Why, oh why, couldn't I have one when it came to love?

"The extended trip to Italy—"

"Business," I interrupted.

"This TV show—"

"More business."

"You're getting a little Martha Stewart, aren't you? What's next, your own pasta channel?"

"That's a good idea, actually."

"It seems to me that your interests are broadening," said Stu.

"You make it sound like that's a bad thing."

"Not at all. But wouldn't you like a little capital to pursue those interests?"

I took another sip of water. "How much capital are we talking?"

Stu reached for his briefcase, unzipped it, pulled out a packet file, and handed it to me. "Here's our proposal."

I opened it and read the cover sheet. The offer was a fifty percent markup over Pasta Pronto's last valuation. You'd think I'd just read a menu rather than a shitload of zeros following a handsome prime number.

"And what happens to me?" I asked.

"You're in charge. No layoffs."

I narrowed my eyes. *Famous last words.*

Stu read my mind and held up his index and middle fingers seemingly glued together. "Scout's honor."

"Like hell you were ever a scout," I said. Stu laughed heartily.

"No bullshit, Katie. I want your company healthy, and I want to keep it healthy. And intact. We want Pasta Pronto to be a Happy Brand. It's a good marriage."

I'd grown rather jaded about marriage.

"I'll have my team look it over and get back to you. But Stu, this is a small town. If I get one whiff of a hostile takeover, I will own your ass."

Stu grinned as if I'd just complimented his tie. Gisela brought our orders to the table. He took one bite of the gnocchi, and his eyes told all. "I know, right?" I said. "Fantastic." My crostini didn't disappoint either.

"Thanks for the referral," he said. Then he held up his drink in a toast. "To good food." I nodded and clinked glasses.

———

To even think about selling Pasta Pronto had always been, in my mind, akin to thinking about giving up a child for adoption. I was always going to fight tooth and nail for my baby.

Until I had the stunning realization that it had stopped feeling like my baby and more like a carnival ride I'd outgrown.

Was this the way out, the answer to my questions? Was it time to reinvent Katie Cravens? Could I sell Pasta Pronto and be done with it? Could I give it up so easily? What would I do otherwise? And what would happen to A Taste of Genoa? How would it affect my relationship with the Caramellis? Did I even have a relationship with either one of them outside of business? What would Luca think if I sold my company?

Why should I care what Luca thinks?

Back at Pasta Pronto HQ, after reading Stu's proposal cover to cover, I met with my team. "Put together a counter-proposal," I said. "And first one to breathe a word of this never works in this town again, got it?"

Well. Another battle in the pasta wars. Seemed like I was fighting them on all fronts.

twenty~six

In addition to the day-to-day activities of running the company, keeping on top of the spreadsheets for Trattoria Naturale (I arranged for a computer system to be installed and intensive instruction for its users), and practicing for *Pasta Wars*, my team and I put together a counter proposal for Stu Chutney and Happy Brands. Although still undecided about whether I wanted to sell Pasta Pronto, I weighed the pros and cons with Cass, happy to have her as a sounding board. If I sold the company and stayed on, I would lose that personal and literal sense of ownership, reduced to an employee rather than a leader or its founder, and that wouldn't work for me. If I sold the company and left, I had no idea what to do in its place, although I'd be financially free to explore some options.

Perhaps that was what I really needed—time to figure out what I wanted. It used to all be so clear.

If I didn't sell, then business would carry on as usual. Or would it? The more time I spent with Cass and consulted with Luci about rethinking "A Taste of Genoa" as an organic pasta line rather than a frozen or processed food (we were even considering a new name—"Buona Fortuna"), the less I believed in the current Pasta Pronto product, and how long before that secret leaked out into the cracks and crevices of everything I touched?

But did I really want to let go? Would it be possible to fall in love with my product again?

I had considered a similar question when I used to fantasize about Max admitting he'd been wrong and begging me to take him back. I'd come to realize that I never wanted him back. I just wanted him to want me back. That's always what hurts more—them not wanting you anymore. They move on so quickly, so easily, as if you meant nothing to them. As if their memory of you was erased. It hurts more than the original wrongdoing, I think, and it's what you never really get over.

———

Luci and Luca arrived in New York earlier in the week for the *Pasta Wars* taping. I offered my home to Luci as repayment for her hospitality in Genoa, but she respectfully declined. More "boundaries," I figured. Or had I misread her in the beginning? I'd thought I was getting an ally as much as a partner. Even a friend. She'd certainly treated me like one when we'd first met. Was that her way of getting others to let their guard down? Or had my entanglement with Luca driven a permanent wedge between his sister and me?

When reporters flat-out asked if she were Team Caramelli or Team Cravens, she offered a benevolent smile and said she was "Team Pasta." The press, of course, interpreted that whichever ways brought the most tension—a split between the Caramelli twins, or a lack of faith in her new business partner.

"I'm sorry you're caught in the middle," I said to her.

"Luca and I are used to it," she replied. "There was a lot of ugliness when we opened and closed the other restaurants. A lot of feuding with our parents became public. Our grandparents had always intended to leave the business to Luca and me. Our parents had felt slighted. It's all okay now—in fact, I think they're glad to be out of it, enjoying their retirement—but I learned it's best to not take any of it personally."

How could I not take all those things Luca said about me personally? Luci said Luca had sworn up and down that he'd never said them, but as Jennifer read me the list of messages following a product development meeting, she hesitated at the last one, as if I was going to shoot the messenger. "And . . . a reporter from the Ultimate Foodie blog asked what you had to say about Chef Caramelli's comment that he hoped there would be EMTs on standby in case the judges needed them after tasting your food."

She actually ducked when she saw my face ravaged in rage.

Through clenched teeth, I replied, "You tell them that the medical team will be needed to tend to Chef Caramelli's ass, which will be severely bruised due to the kicking it's going to get."

"Um, you sure? You don't want to cool off?"

Screw civility. Screw sportsmanship. Screw Luca.

"No. If it's war he wants, then it's war he gets. Go on, do it. No, you know what? I'll do it myself. After all, *I* fight my own battles."

And those were the final shots fired until Luca and I came face to face at the press event the night before the competition.

Wendy spent the entire morning prepping me for the two o'clock press conference. I'd purchased a new dress a la Jessica Pearson from *Suits*—not surprised to discover I'd gone up two dress sizes, yet pleasantly surprised by how muscular my body had become and how the dress seemed to hug it in all the right places. A stylist perfected my hair and makeup. Standing before a full-length mirror, I observed the reflection. *This isn't a woman who sends drunk texts and dumps boiling water on her foot and falls off bicycles. This is a woman who makes sound business decisions, who commits to something—or someone—and sticks to that commitment. This is a woman* in control.

I must have gone to the bathroom four times in the thirty minutes before the press conference. I felt nauseous. Woozy. Panicky. Like my knees were going to buckle. Like my tongue would stick to the roof of my mouth. Like my brain was set to malfunction in three . . . two . . . one . . .

Yeah. Katie Cravens in control.

The PR team and I entered the pressroom to find it mocked up as a boxing ring, where Luca and I were expected to face off in the middle and all the reporters and photographers would flood around the ropes. More like being caged animals on display at a zoo. So demeaning. Who on Wendy's team thought this was a good idea, or even original, for that matter?

"I want chairs," I said.

"Excuse me?" said Wendy's assistant.

"I am not standing in this stupid contraption to be gawked at without a podium or something to ground me. Either get two chairs or two podiums or cancel this thing."

"But—"

"I don't care about the visual. Get two chairs or I'm out of here. *Capisce?*"

Within minutes two director's chairs with mini-microphones were brought into the ring, accompanied by a little table between them set with two bottles of water. I approved.

"Now remember all the trash-talking Gianluca has done," coached Wendy. I half-expected her to stand behind me and rub my shoulders like a manager warming up her prizefighter. "Keep your guard up, and feel free to get in a little jab here and there, because let's face it, that's why we're here. It's not personal; it's just all part of the game. Good clean fun."

Good clean fun???

It suddenly occurred to me that I had yet to have fun.

And then he appeared.

The thick shock of hair and the obsidian eyes and the sharp cheekbones and the olive-toned skin (I suddenly wondered whether that was the product of his eating so many olives). Dressed in the familiar blue jeans and oxfords and bandana and chef's jacket—my guess was that some publicist told him to do that—but he still looked extraordinary. Like Superman.

I wanted him. God, I wanted to rip open that chef's jacket and pull off his clothes and do him right there in that boxing ring. Just wrestle him to the floor and take him. And yet, I also wanted to beat him senseless with a whisk.

I watched him take in the sight of me—brunette, curvier, professionally put together—and his eyes widened with surprise and even bewilderment.

Breathe deeply.

"Hello, Luca," I said, trying to sound professional rather than jilted.

He stood motionless, seemingly unable to speak.

I filled in the awkward silence. "Thank you for agreeing to do this gig. I know how you hate this sellout stuff. Been great for business, however. It'll be great for the new pasta line too."

He was just about to attempt speech when I heard a familiar voice call my name.

Luciana and Cass approached me, and each took turns to greet me.

"You look fit and healthy and vibrant," said Luci. "*Molto bella*. And I love your new hair color, or should I say, your original hair color?"

"More or less," I said.

"You look like *you* now."

My heart filled like a balloon. Perhaps Luci and I could become friends after all? Was it worth sacrificing a business relationship to do so, and maybe even the deal itself? Or would that be Stu Chutney's problem?

"Thank you, Luci," I said. "I'm glad you're here."

Cass nudged me toward Luca. "Looks like I'm not the only one who thinks you're a vision."

Luci's brow furrowed. "I hope you two get a chance to talk when this whole thing is done. You both really need it."

Being alone with Luca was the last thing I wanted. Or rather, the thing I wanted most. Thus, it could never happen. Ever.

Wendy announced the beginning of the press conference. Luca and I took our seats and Wendy's team helped us clip our mics to our clothing unobtrusively. Luca opened one of the bottles of water and swigged from it like a beer. He looked tense, stiff, turned off. Toby Ashford, our twenty-two-year-old celebrity MC and former member of the boy band The Buzz, stepped into the ring, shook hands with both of us, and, like a boxing referee, introduced Luca and me with all the drama and exaggeration and cornball puns one could blather, all scripted. *Seriously? Who planned this shit?*

The Q and A began:

Q: How are you feeling about the competition tomorrow, Katie?

ME: I'm as ready as I can be.

Q: Chef Caramelli, do you think you have a worthy opponent in Katie Cravens?

LUCA: If she wasn't, I wouldn't be here.

Don't read into his answers, don't read into his answers, don't read into his answers. . . .

Seriously, though, did he just compliment me?

Q: Miss Cravens, do you think you really have a chance to beat Chef Caramelli?

ME: I don't know. All I know is that it's not about who wins or loses. It's about having fun and making some delicious pasta. That's what I want to focus on. That, and doing my best, getting a chance to show off what I've learned.

From the corner of my eye, I saw the corner of Luca's mouth twitch upward, as if he were concealing a smile, and my insides fluttered.

The press was getting antsy. Wendy was downright annoyed. Clearly I was not heeding her advice about remembering all the pot shots Luca had taken at me and jabbing a few of my own. He and I had never held back before; so what was all the dancing around each other about? What happened to my wanting to crush him?

Q: Chef Caramelli, do you still think Pasta Pronto is "microwave bastardization," and if so, then why did you approve of your family's upcoming specialty pasta line that you and Pasta Pronto are collaborating on?

Luca took another gulp from the bottle, presumably to buy him some time to consider his answer.

LUCA: I've already stated that I won't be involved in this project. However, I trust that Miss Cravens and my sister will come up with something that will honor the Caramelli name.

Miss Cravens? Yuck. Luca looked as if he'd rather be doing something more productive, like alligator wrestling or attending a paint-drying convention.

Q: Chef Caramelli, do you want to beat Katie Cravens tomorrow?

Luca looked at the reporter quizzically. "I want to win," he said matter-of-factly.

Q: So, you *do* want to beat her.

LUCA: No, I want to *win*.

We were losing our audience with our pacifist responses. Too diplomatic and circumspect. Wendy had a point—conflict sells. Thus, I went for the left hook.

"*I* want to beat him," I blurted. Luca whipped his head in my direction and glowered at me, but I steadied my attention front and center.

Q: But you just said—

"I know what I said. I lied. I want to crush him. He's been talking trash for weeks now, and tomorrow I'm going to put him in his place. I'm going to take down the almighty Gianluca Caramelli."

"What do you have to say to that, Chef Caramelli?" asked the reporter.

I flung a little more gas onto the fire. "Yeah, Luca. What do you have to say?"

Luca narrowed his eyes at me, and shook his head in that condescending, patronizing, exasperated way I'd seen so many times before.

"I'd like to see you try," he said.

"I've come a long way since Alba," I said to him, suddenly forgetting about the gaggle of reporters and photographers in the room. "I think you're in for quite a surprise tomorrow."

"I don't care if you studied with the best," he started. "I don't care if you studied with *me*. You'll never be as good as I am, Miss Katie. You can't be. You don't have the heart of a chef."

"I know the secret ingredient," I said.

Luca was taken aback as simultaneous shouts of "What's the secret ingredient?" and "Will you use the secret ingredient tomorrow?" fired off. His pupils dilated and his irises clouded and his brow furrowed in fearful recoil, not unlike that night in Genoa.

"You know nothing," he said to me under his breath, although I'm sure the mic picked it up.

"I know more than you think," I said. "I know more than you ever will about it."

Luca unclipped his mic, hopped off the chair, cursed in Italian, looked me square in the eye, and said, "I'm going to bury you tomorrow," before walking out.

Stay calm, stay calm, stay calm, I told my trembling self as I watched Luci follow her brother, and I instantly regretted every word I said. Toby Ashford attempted to save the awkward moment by tossing out another canned pun, and then thanked everyone for coming.

Wendy rushed up to me. "Good job," she said as I yanked the mic from my dress and threw it on the chair.

"Are you kidding me? That was a disaster."

"It's war," said Wendy.

"I thought you said it was a game. Make up your mind, will you? Because it's a lousy way to sell pasta." I stormed out and back to my office, where I spent the remainder of the day staring out the window, replaying every word of the Q and A in my head, and desperately wishing for a do-over.

twenty~seven

Given that I had to be at the Flavor Channel television studios so early for preparation and taping the following morning, I booked a room at the same hotel Luci and Luca were staying rather than go all the way back to Dix Hills. Once settled, I rode the escalator up two floors, paraded down the hall, knocked on Luca's door three times, and waited.

The door flung open, and I took in a full-frontal view of Luca, shirtless in all his six-pack-ab glory.

He scowled at me. "What are you doing here?"

I barged past him into his room. "It's time we have it out, Luca. You can start by telling me why you dumped me in Genoa and then agreed to do this show."

"I think I made that perfectly clear at the time," he replied. "And I did you a favor by agreeing to this stupid, childish thing. But all you've done is insult me and call me names and—"

"Me? *You're* the one who started it!"

"I never said a word."

"Are you really going to stand here and deny that you said I can't boil water without injuring myself and that you hoped there would be EMTs in case the judges got sick and that there wouldn't be any microwaves? Who else would say such things? Who else would be so rude and cruel and heartless?"

"*Not me*," he said. "I should've been done with you, Miss Katie."

"Like you were done with me that night at the villa? Like you were done with the Caramelli restaurants? Like you'll be done with Alberto once you spend him out of house and home? Like you were done when—" I cut myself off.

But he knew. He knew what I was going to say. *When Vincenzo died.*

It was as if I'd just slapped him, and he reeled from the pain. "You know nothing—*nothing*!" he shouted. "You don't know me. You don't know my sister. You didn't know my grandfather." He breathed hard as his eyes filled with glassy tears. "You didn't *know* him!"

But I wanted to. I wanted to know everything.

I took hold and cupped his face in my hands. "Feed me, Luca," I pleaded, kissed him hard, and let go of all control.

twenty~eight

There are two kinds of people in this world: "pantsers" and "planners." A pantser is someone who flies by the seat of their pants, goes where the wind takes them, and gets by in life with very little planning or organization. Planners, on the other hand, are self-explanatory. I am a planner. Always have been. I live by calendars and appointment books and lists and bulletin boards and post-it notes and Siri reminders and alarm clocks and wake-up calls. Luca, on the other hand, is a total pantser. He comes and goes as he pleases, doesn't wear a watch, and makes decisions as if they have no consequences. He doesn't even use measuring cups or spoons when he cooks.

I'm not sure which is the most deadly combination in terms of coupling: two planners (me and Max), two pantsers (Luca and probably every woman he's ever been with), or a planner and a pantser.

I sat up straight in bed, the room still dark, and realized what had just happened. I mean, *of course* I knew what happened: Luca and I had sex. Lots of sex. Lots of ecstatic, fantasmic, clutching-the-headboard, bilingual orgasm-riddled sex.

Oh yeah. Luca finished this time. He finished me too.

The reality check was, specifically, that we'd had sex mere hours before we had to face off against each other in the *Pasta Wars* competition. How was I going to be able to concentrate on cooking when Luca and I pretty much just binged on each other's bodies? How was I to treat him as a formidable opponent when he'd whispered things like *bella mia* and *torta dolce* and *splendida rosa* after nibbling on my earlobes? How was I supposed to think *crush him* in the kitchen when all I wanted to do was douse his naked body with powdered sugar and cover him with strawberry jam?

To say nothing of the fact that after today, one of us was going to be a winner and the other a loser. One of us was going to walk away humiliated, beaten by the other, and let's face it—it was going to be me. I didn't stand a chance against Luca in the kitchen. He was Iron Chef material when it came to all things pasta.

Why couldn't we at least have waited until after the competition to have sex? How could I have been so thoughtless, so pantser-like?

Luca stirred and murmured something inaudible.

"I have to go," I said, and slid out from underneath the covers.

Luca groggily tried to grab my arm, but I slipped away too quickly. "Nooooooo, Miss Katie." He beckoned. "Don't go."

I went on a scavenger hunt for my clothes as I spoke. "Luca, in just a few short hours we have to be mortal enemies. Not to mention I have to cook something that won't make the judges ask for a barf bag. How on earth am I possibly going to do that now? What were we thinking? We weren't thinking. See, this is what happens when I don't think. This is what happens when I let go of my senses. I do stupid things. Crazy, stupid things. Now I have to fool the world into thinking I know what I'm doing and that I'm not a sex-crazed lunatic who sleeps with the competition as some sort of psychological warfare—oh, God, was that what this was? Did you do this on purpose, Luca? No, wait. You couldn't have. I came to you. *Ugggghhh!!!*"

I didn't even realize that I'd stopped talking to Luca and started talking to myself, oblivious to the fact that he heard every word.

He interjected into my verbal stream of consciousness. "I wasn't trying to gain an edge. I would never do such a thing. Not like this. And not by saying things to the press. You know I didn't say those things, right?"

"Whatever," I replied, not paying attention as I bundled the rest of my things in a frenzy. "I have a million things to do."

Luca slid out of bed. "Katie," he said as I was at the door. "Wait."

I stopped and stood and impatiently tapped my foot.
"What?"

He came chin to chin with me and caressed my cheek with the back of his hand, and my tapping foot was replaced by a hot pulsing elsewhere. I closed my eyes and let the flash of heat run through me and temporarily soften every clenched muscle.

"This wasn't a mistake," he said above a whisper.

I opened my eyes and looked in his, seeing dejection. "Luca . . ." I started, but there was just too much to say. An inordinate number of reasons why we shouldn't have slept together, regardless of how good it felt and how much I wanted to again, scrolled across my mind like a marquee, directly contrasting all the girlish fantasies of us riding off into the sunset in Luca's Ferrari. It would be so easy to give in to that fantasy, to leave Pasta Pronto and New York City and my empty Dix Hills home and mergers and deadlines and stockholders behind. To go with the wind.

But that wasn't me. I needed structure. I needed organization. I needed a plan.

"I really have to go, Luca," I said, and left without even kissing him good-bye. I couldn't. If I did, my pants would have come off again, literally and figuratively.

Two shampoos, one conditioning treatment, a good soaping, and hibiscus-scented lotion, powder, and three body spritzes later, I could still smell him on me.

I was so completely screwed.

---

arrived at the studio wearing jeans, a T-shirt, and running shoes with good traction, given that I'd probably be racing around the kitchen just like you saw on all those cooking competition shows. I'd come early enough to take a tour of the studio kitchens and become familiar with my workspace and where everything was. The pasta maker was at a separate station, just like in Trattoria Naturale. Heather Lawrence, the producer, told me that we'd prepare batches of dough now so they would be ready for use later, and then be filmed making one batch live. Thus, the dough we'd be taking out of the fridge to run in the pasta maker would be the premade dough rather than the one we'd just put in.

So much for reality television.

"You'll be told thirty minutes prior to the start of the competition what you'll be making," said Heather. "That's rather generous; the Iron Chefs get much less time than that. You can consult with your coach at that point if you want, but you can't look anything up or use a recipe."

"No one told me I could have a coach present," I said. Cass had told me that she'd be busy filming her own show, but the *Pasta Wars* crew might call her in for a post-production appearance.

Clearly I was on my own.

Luca was already fifteen minutes late. Where the heck was he? Should I call him right now? Text him? Tell him to get his ass over here *pronto*?

Just as an irked production assistant ordered me to start prepping my pasta dough, Luca ambled in wearing similar attire as me, albeit a much tighter T-shirt, carrying his chef's jacket and bandana. Unshaven. Was he going for sexy, or I-don't-give-a-shit? Both were plausible. Just seeing him sent my heart pounding, my blood coursing, my entire pelvic region aflame. The hairs on my arms stood up. Goose bumps broke out. My heartbeat sprinted.

He wouldn't even glance in my direction.

I'd hurt him. This morning, when I'd babbled on about how thoughtless I'd been, how stupid it was . . . talk about thoughtless and stupid . . .

Or maybe he was ignoring me in an effort to hide from others that we'd spent the night doing the horizontal tango? Was he putting on a game face? Was he trying to psych me out? Was he making an effort to focus on the competition? After all, he had way more to lose than I did. He had a reputation to uphold. Maybe he resented being here, having denounced shows and spectacles such as these all along. But if that were the case, then why had he said yes to it in the first place?

Or maybe he'd internalized my post-sex panic—which I was desperate to retract—and agreed that yes, it had been a stupid thing to do. Maybe he regretted the day I set foot in Trattoria Naturale, regretted ever hearing the name Katie Cravens. Maybe all he wanted was a one-way ticket back to Alba.

Yes, it had to be that. And I couldn't blame him.

I tried not to obsessively stare or eavesdrop as Heather Lawrence hastily filled Luca in on the pasta dough prep and the rundown on taping, but I couldn't help myself; Luca couldn't have looked more disinterested than if someone were reading him the back of a cereal box.

If this was the way he was going to be, then screw it. I didn't have time to worry. I had pasta dough to make and a competition to win. I had a business to think about. Or at least that's what I told myself.

My hands shook so much I nearly dropped one egg and missed the flour well with the other. And we weren't even filming or in front of an audience yet. Thirty minutes prior to filming, as promised, a production assistant named John called Luca and me to the side of the stage and revealed the game plan:

ROUND ONE: Good ol' spaghetti and meatballs.

ROUND TWO: Carbonara. How we made it was up to us.

ROUND THREE: I'd have to go head-to-head making Luca's signature dish: ravioli stuffed with ricotta cheese, zucchini, ground sausage, and dried spices, and topped with a sun-dried tomato sauce.

The last one wasn't a "signature" dish as much as something Luca created at Caramelli's to "appease the Americans," despite being advertised on the menu otherwise. The entire lineup was ridiculously Americanized, in fact. Funny how I wouldn't have noticed three months ago. Wouldn't have even known such a notion existed. Clearly they were going easy on me—no tortellini, no gnocchi, no shells, nothing that required true skill or mastery. At least I had a halfway decent shot with the ravioli given that I had studied the Caramelli's menu after returning from Genoa and it was one of the recipes Luci sent after my session with Cass.

A gallery of people filed in, with Luci and her assistant Rosa sitting in the front row. My first time seeing Luci since the previous day's press conference, I avoided her, uncertain of what to say or whether she would speak to me. Had she seen her brother in the last few hours? Had she been in the hotel room next door and heard our outbursts of passion?

A production assistant approached me. "How are you?" she asked.

"I might pass out," I replied.

The assistant handed me a sheet of paper, folded in threes, like a subpoena. "I work on Cass Brophy's show. She asked me to give you this message."

I unfolded what turned out to be stationary with Flavor Channel letterhead and read, in bold, loopy handwriting:

Dear Katie—

Ignore everyone. Rather than cooking for the judges, pretend you're cooking for one person. Someone you love. Someone you trust. Someone who feeds your heart.

I'm rooting for you.

Love, Cass

My eyes welled up. There was only one person—not Max, who took my trust, or my parents, who took away the ability to love my body or see food as something more than a complicated relationship—one person who pushed all my buttons and aimed his expletives at me and could cook me under the table. But he also made food something intimate with me. He kissed and caressed me with the passion of an artist.

And yet, for some reason cooking for Luca seemed even more daunting than cooking for three people who wanted nothing more than to find fault with my food.

Did I love Luca? Did I trust him? Did he feed my heart? He certainly fed my body—in more ways than one.

One by one, the judges took their seats:

Gene Melton, author of the cookbook *Chalkboard Menu, Washboard Abs* and co-owner in both diner and gym franchises. Could potentially be in my corner, although he also looked like he and Luca could appear on the cover of *GQ* together, or in *People*'s Sexiest Man Alive issue.

Louis Bensa, owner of the restaurant *Bensa!* in East Hampton, host of an online cooking show, *Buon Appetito with Bensa*, and launching his own line of cookware in the fall. He made eye contact with and smiled at me as he sat down (maybe *I* should cook for him, I thought).

Finally, Sofia Antonio-Feretti, executive editor of *CRAVE* magazine and one of Pasta Pronto's fiercest critics.

Little windmills turned and churned my stomach. I felt woozy. Nauseous. Like someone turned up the temperature in the studio by thirty degrees—or was that because Luca was standing no more than ten feet away from me in the adjacent kitchen?

I was given a plain white chef's jacket with short sleeves, and I admit that the instant I put it on, I felt dichotomously legitimate and fraudulent. Luca wore his usual slate blue chef's jacket with the bandana, and he looked so sexy I thought I might need to wear those horse blinder thingies to keep myself from looking at him. Luca had vehemently refused to do the "documentary" interview format, which kind of relieved me, so the format was going to be more of *Iron Chef* and less *Chopped*.

They filmed Toby Ashford making the introductions of us and the judges first, and Marty Melnick, the director, kept trying to goad Luca and me into looking "tough": arms crossed in defiance, badass poses, ferocious eyes. The most they could get out of Luca was mild annoyance; from me, masked terror.

After the introductions and rules, Toby declared: "Let the *Pasta Wars* begin!"

Frightening words, indeed.

twenty~nine

Toby "surprised" us with round one: spaghetti and meatballs. We had forty minutes to make it, which was oodles of time in the food competition world. Of course, in dramatic fashion, the moment Toby announced: "Time starts *NOW*," Luca and I broke into mad dashes for the pantry and fridge to hunt and gather everything we needed: flour, eggs, meat, produce, herbs and spices. As we awkwardly bumped into each other trying to collect everything in one trip, I whispered a "Sorry" to him, uncertain if I was apologizing for blocking his path or this morning's rant, which I was still aching to recant. Merely touching him via our sleeves sent little flares of heat up and down my spine. He continued to ignore me, which rattled me even further.

Back at my kitchen and looking at everything set out in front of me, I suddenly panicked as they morphed into foreign objects. *What is this? Who are all these people? What am I doing here???* I became further petrified as I heard Judge Gene say, "She's not choking already, is she?" Glancing at Luca, I saw him casually beating the eggs within the flour well and getting ready to take over with his hands. Already?

Do something, Katie, an inner voice demanded.

On the verge of tears and contemplating running offstage, I caught a glimpse of Cass—who had told me she was going to try to poke her head in at some point, but had made no promises—off to the side, looking straight at me, pointing to her heart.

Cook for one person. Someone you love. Someone who feeds your heart.

At that moment, a wave of calm washed over me as I came back to myself. I grabbed a measuring cup and scooped out equal parts all-purpose and semolina flour, whisked them together with my fingers, and made the flour well, to which I expertly cracked two eggs and added pinches of salt and a drizzle of olive oil (I'd been previously measuring, but on a whim decided to try it by sight). Luca was already kneading his dough into a perfect sheen of a ball while I was slowly pulling flour into the egg mixture, working methodically while still aware of the time ticking away on the ominous digital clock lording over us. I was focused now, a dish of spaghetti and meatballs forming a perfect picture in my mind's eye.

When I finished my dough and put it in the fridge (our premade dough labeled and resting patiently for us), I went to work on the meatballs. Luca was way ahead of me, already shaping about a dozen meatballs and placing half of them into a pot of oil before working on a dozen more. *Two dozen meatballs!* Was he crazy? Showing off? But then I realized, each judge would expect at least two meatballs, if not three, plus a plate for Toby, and one for my opponent. So yeah, two dozen meatballs was suddenly very plausible. Given that fifteen minutes had already passed, I would have to take my chances on just one dozen.

Using Cass's recipe, I combined ground sirloin, pork, and veal; panko; finely chopped fresh parsley; dried oregano; salt and pepper; and an egg, and dug my hands in to combine it all. The mixture was cold and squishy, little bits wedging under my fingernails, but I persisted, until I realized, *Shit! I forgot to take out the baking sheet before I immersed my hands into raw meat ick! And preheat the oven!* Which meant I had to stop what I was doing, wash my hands, turn on the oven (I raised the temperature by 25 degrees), grab a baking sheet, place it next to the bowl, form the meatballs and place them one by one on the sheet, and wash my hands again before drizzling the meatballs with olive oil, the blasted clock ticking down my doom all the while.

Judge Sofia commented on my strategy: "She's going to bake them? That's a bit of a risk."

Ignore them, an inner voice said. *You're not making it for them.*

Oh yeah? countered yet another inner voice. *Remember that when they give you zero points for being a loser.*

Now what? Should I start the sauce, or make the pasta?

I glanced at Luca chopping an onion at warp speed.

Start the sauce.

My chopping skills had improved tenfold since my days with Luca in Alba, but I was still slow. I needed to chop a whole onion, two carrots, several cloves of garlic, and four San Marzano tomatoes with approximately twenty minutes remaining. I also needed to sauté the onions, carrots, and garlic, then puree them with the tomatoes.

Not to mention make the pasta.

Holy frappe.

The onion burned my eyes so bad tears came gushing down my cheeks. Marty Melnick hollered at someone to stop the clock. Luca and I stopped what we were doing as well.

"We can't have ten minutes of Katie weeping over her onion," said Marty. To me, he commanded, "Finish chopping. We'll edit. Then clean yourself up and restart the clock." To Luca, he said, "Stop what you're doing until we resume."

Wasn't that cheating?

I sobbed and wiped my eyes with the back of my hand, surely smearing mascara, and pointed to Luca. "It's not fair to give me a handicap over him. He should keep working as well."

Without waiting for Marty's approval, Luca did just that by reaching for a skillet, twirling it like a baton, and placing it on a burner.

"Damn," said Marty. "I wish we'd caught that."

Seemingly impatient, everyone watched and waited for me to finishing cutting up the stupid onion. Their eyes burned into me like lasers as I sliced and diced and sniffled and sobbed and tried not to let any tears drip on the cutting board or the onion. Not only that, but I turned beet-red with embarrassment. No more than a few minutes passed, but I could have sworn the sun had already set.

"Okay," I finally announced. "I'm done."

"Let's get a shot of one final chop of the onion, have Katie go off to the side and dry off, and then start the clock again," barked Marty. "And for God's sake, don't put the camera on *that*," he said of the clock.

On the call of *Action*, I ran my knife through the chopped onions and then rushed to the side to wipe down my face with a towel miraculously waiting for me, careful not to take my makeup off with the tears—although between my nerves and the sweltering lights I was already drenched underneath the chef's jacket, certain I'd sweated out five pounds, and guessing my face was looking pretty pasty.

Luca looked like the Robin Thicke of chefs—calm and cool and collected. He looked like he couldn't be bothered with any of it. I actually missed his Italian profanity rants. I would have preferred it to his apathy.

When I ran back to my station, the clock started again. I must have eaten up at least seven minutes, every one of them like currency I'd just been spared.

And yet, I believed it to be completely unfair and unsportsmanlike. In fact, the entire competition was beginning to feel like a sham. Or rather, *I* was feeling like a sham—as a cook, a contestant, even as a CEO.

I flung the vegetables into the skillet, hastily sautéed them, and dumped them in the food processor with the chopped tomatoes. Rather than turn on the processor, however, the restarted clock signaled that it was time for me to get to work on the pasta, which I did. Luckily that was the one area I'd mastered, and I confidently, skillfully ran the premade dough through the pasta maker, transforming it into spaghetti. A pot of water already sat on a burner, and I couldn't for the life of me figure out how it manifested. Had it been there before we started taping, and I never noticed? Had a production assistant placed it there while I was drying off from my onion-weepfest? Had I fetched it at the word *GO* with the other supplies and ingredients and forgotten?

I flicked on the burner and rushed to the oven to check on the meatballs. As I cut into one, I heard Judge Gene say, "That's a no-no. She should be testing their doneness with a meat thermometer, not cutting one open. She can't serve that one now. She just wasted a meatball," while Judge Sofia followed with, "She shouldn't have to test them at all."

Shit. They didn't look done, though. And where was the meat thermometer?

Luca's meatballs sat on a towel absorbing the excess oil as he tossed chopped tomatoes in the skillet with a flick of his wrist, like all the professional chefs do. God, I would so rather be watching Luca cook than darting about in a frenzied sweat with damp, frizzy flyaways falling out of my ponytail and a pasty face and hoping I wouldn't overcook the meatballs now that I couldn't cut another one open and didn't have time to look for a meat thermometer.

When the water reached the boiling point, I dropped the spaghetti in handfuls at a time. *Watch the clock*, I reminded myself. *It will be done before you know it, and you don't want to serve him soggy pasta.*

And sure enough, I barely had time to finish the pureeing the sauce in the food processor before the pasta needed to come out of the pot. Rather than drain and risk spilling water again, burning a hole right through my foot this time, I found a pronged spoon and removed the spaghetti several spoon-fuls at a time, like I had seen Alberto and Luca do at Trattoria Naturale.

"Time to plate!" Toby called out. Luca was already meticulously arranging the sauce-infused spaghetti in swirls with tongs and spooning more chunky tomato sauce on top of a pyramid of meatballs and garnishing them with whole basil leaves.

What was I thinking, pureeing my sauce? Major time suck. And the meatballs were probably done. Hopefully done. (*Please, please, let them be done!*) I yanked them out of the oven and accidentally slammed the door shut, causing a loud bang that made several people wince, myself included. I yelled out "Sorry!" and hoped they'd edit.

Hang on, Katie.

I ran a successful, publicly traded company. I worked under pressure all the time. And what made me so good? I problem-solved. I multitasked.

I can do this.

Activate multitask Katie.

The remaining five minutes happened in a blur: spaghetti in plates (my swirls ended up being collapsed piles). Ample servings of pureed tomato sauce on top. Two meatballs arranged side by side, only to keep rolling off the spaghetti like runaway billiard balls. A little more sauce on the meatballs. I wiped down the edges of the plates with a clean towel and tried to reposition the meatballs.

"TWENTY SECONDS!"

Garnish! Garnish!

Panicked, I looked left and right. Nothing.

Parmesan cheese! I dashed to a hunk of Parmigiano Reggiano sitting on Luca's counter and grabbed it along with the grater next to it as everyone counted down the final seconds, their voices ringing in my ears like clashing gongs.

"TIME'S UP!"

Shit. No cheese. No garnish at all.

Holy freakin' frappe. And that was only course one. I still had two more to go.

Feeling the moisture of sweat as I buried my face in my hands, I swallowed back every emotion I had and staunched the pool of welling tears, not an onion in sight.

I looked at Luca, who, for the first time, showed affect in his eyes, as if he were desperate to comfort me, but was invisibly chained and fenced in his kitchen.

thirty

Time to feed the judges.

While Marty directed the camera crew to take close-ups of our plates specifically prepared for that purpose, John the production assistant escorted me to the side of the soundstage for a hair and makeup redo, a bottle of water (I downed half of it in seconds), and a blast of cool air.

"You okay, Miss Cravens?" asked the assistant. "You look a little pale. Have you eaten anything today?"

I honestly couldn't remember. My dazed look must have been affirmative, because he came back with a hunk of Italian bread from the set. "Here," he said as he maniacally tore off a piece. "Have some." I bit into it, but my mouth was so dry it was like chewing paper, and my throat closed up, barely allowing me to swallow.

I handed the bread back to him. "Thank you," I said, and downed the rest of the water.

Luca came to me with a cold compress and dabbed my forehead. The gesture was so tender, so unexpected. Oh, to just fall into his arms right then and there. . . .

I didn't deserve it.

I closed my eyes and imagined myself in a spa-like bathtub, with Luca fanning me with palm fronds. *No—scratch that. Luca is in the tub with me and . . .*

This fantasy was doing little to cool me down.

"Thank you," I said to him, and exhaled an exhausted, frustrated sigh. "I thought this was supposed to be good clean fun. That was one of the most stressful hours of my life, and I've been in some pretty stressful board meetings."

"The second round will be easier," he said.

"I'm looking forward to tasting your spaghetti, although I already know it'll taste fantabulous. Mine looks like slop on a plate."

"You took a risk baking the meatballs. That's good. Judges like risks."

"Their comments indicated otherwise. And I doubt they like risks that fail."

"How do you know it failed?"

"I don't know. But I forgot to taste one to see if it was okay. I forgot to taste everything, come to think of it."

Luca didn't respond, and I figured it was his way of agreeing that I screwed up without having to come out and say it, despite the latter having always been his way. We'd been avoiding eye contact, but we locked in for just a second. "Luca . . ." I started. But before I could say anything else, the production assistants hurried us back onto the soundstage.

Luca faced the judges first, who praised the taste:

"Your pasta is cooked perfectly."

"These meatballs are divine."

"I wouldn't call this sauce 'traditional,' but it's delicious."

He won kudos for presentation as well. They criticized him, however, on "playing it safe."

Judge Sofia leered at Luca with cat eyes. "You can make this for me anytime," she purred. I expected her to place her thumb and pinky to her ear in a telephone-like gesture and mouth *Call me* to him.

Luca barely nodded his head in acknowledgment, and didn't say a word in response to any of the judges' comments. Toby, irked by Luca's indifference, asked him some questions to try to get him to talk. Luca replied in Italian, irking him even more. Toby looked in Marty's direction offstage and said, "Geezus, really?" I would have laughed had I not wanted to drop. Rude to the end.

"We'll subtitle it," said Marty. "It's good television."

Something told me there'd be no subtitles, though. At least none permitted on basic cable television.

Next, they put the camera on me holding the plate. I plunged my fork in, twirled the pasta around it, and quickly brought the fork to my mouth so that I wouldn't wind up slurping spaghetti strands. I closed my eyes as I chewed, just as I always did eating Luca's food. It was good. Basil-y. I expressed approval with an "Mmmmmm" before slicing into a meatball with my fork and tasting that as well.

Wow.

"Ohmigod, that's like the best meatball I've ever eaten," I said. I caught a flicker in Luca's eyes as the corner of his mouth twitched. I looked at Luca. "Thank you," I said, as if he'd made it just for me. He seemed as surprised by my sincerity, and the utterance itself, as I was. Not to mention touched.

My turn to face the judges.

"*Buona sorte*," he said. *Good luck*.

"*Grazie*," I replied, my pronunciation and inflection having improved quite a bit, and stepped away from him to take my place at the marker in front of the judges, inquisition-style.

The judges were polite regarding taste:

"The pasta is well-cooked; perhaps could have been a little more *al dente*."

"I like that you took a risk baking the meatballs, but they're a little dry, which means you overcooked them. Otherwise tasty."

However, they mentioned nothing about presentation. Judge Louis smiled and asked, "Are you nervous?"

I nodded vigorously, unable to find my voice.

"Don't be," he said. "Have fun out there. It's just food. Food is fun."

Luca's voice echoed in my mind: *Il cibo è vita*.

I smiled in gratitude to Judge Louis.

Judge Sofia, however, added, "You need to manage your time a little better."

No shit.

"And your onions," quipped Toby. *Idiot*.

"Okay," I squeaked.

Okay? *Okay???* I should have cursed at them in Italian. I knew all the words now.

I thanked the judges and bowed in reverence to them like they were clergy. Someone handed Luca a plate of my spaghetti. He dipped and twirled his fork, took in a bite, and nodded his head as he chewed.

Oh God, he hates it.

"It's very good," he said.

He's being polite. He'd spit it out if he could.

He repeated with the meatball.

"Perfect seasoning," he said.

Code for "dry."

As if reading my mind, he looked at me intently. "Really, it's good."

Hold me, Luca. Just hold me and kiss me and take me out of here.

"Ready for course two?" asked Toby.

Somebody bean this guy with a skillet, please.

Course two was the carbonara. We were filmed looking "surprised" upon its reveal as Toby pointed to the thirty-minute clock and yelled "Time starts . . . *NOW*," activating my adrenaline once again as I raced back to the fridge to retrieve more pasta dough, grateful we didn't have to make it on the spot again.

Have fun, have fun, have fun, I repeated like a mantra. I'd been thinking about how I wanted to make the carbonara. The judges liked risks. So I decided to go with prosciutto rather than bacon or pancetta, and asparagus to add a bit of color. Cass had turned me on to roasting vegetables—having spent half my life boiling or steaming them, my first time tasting roasted veggies had been a religious experience. Oh, the texture and the *flavor*! I couldn't go back to boiled blandness even if my waistline demanded it—my taste buds became my new overlords.

I prepared the asparagus in a bowl with salt, pepper, garlic powder, olive oil, and a spritz of lemon juice, tossed it all, and transferred it to a baking sheet before placing it in the oven, overhearing the judges' approval, until Judge Sofia pointed out that Luca was doing *the exact same thing*. "Apparently she did her homework on the Caramellis before collaborating with them," she said in a smarmy tone. "She knows their tricks."

I hoped Luca wasn't using prosciutto. I needed an edge.

He'll probably use olives. Or capers.

The smell of bacon wafted over from Luca's kitchen. My stomach growled.

After running the dough through the fettuccine attachment on the pasta maker, I tended to the sauce, searing the prosciutto in olive oil and sautéing garlic cloves in the prosciutto grease for added flavor. I dropped the fettuccine noodles into the pot of boiling water (which again had magically appeared). Next, I beat several eggs and added grated parmesan cheese and yet another dash of lemon juice to mimic the flavor of the asparagus. Minutes later, I transferred the fettuccine to the skillet, removed it from the heat, and switched between adding the egg mixture and the starchy pasta water. I removed the roasted asparagus from the oven, tasted one (*perfecto!*), and added it to the creamy carbonara, garnishing with chopped flat-leaf parsley.

This time I remembered to taste.

Oh my.

Now I'm having a good time.

The intensity of the kitchen matched the intensity of the boardroom. Having realized that, I'd seized the reins and taken control.

With about a minute to spare, I focused on improving the plating presentation—not overloading the portions; making sure no excess sauce dripped around the edges; sprinkling with more fresh parsley and slivers of parmesan cheese.

"Time's up!" yelled Toby. I breathed a sigh of satisfaction.

Again we took a break, but Luca didn't join me in front of the cooling fans this time. Maybe he sensed my confidence, and his competitive spirit was kicking in. Or maybe he remembered how shitty I'd treated him this morning, which was increasingly feeling like a lifetime ago.

Regardless, I missed him there.

At tasting time, the judges were more critical of Luca's dish, the presentation of which looked so beautiful one could snap a photo with a smartphone and it would look like a magazine-caliber photo. Not to mention you could probably eat the photo and still taste the real thing.

"Delicious," they all said, "but predictable."

Seriously?

"I thought you of all people would have used *guanciale* instead of bacon," said Judge Gene.

I'd learned about guanciale. They were pork jowls. Ew.

"Last time I did things my way in the States, the customers didn't approve," said Luca.

"Surely you're not comparing our palates to the average restaurant patron's," said Judge Gene on behalf of his fellow insulted judges.

Luca made a face that implied, *Well . . .*

If I didn't know any better, I'd swear Judge Gene was about to challenge Luca to his own pasta throwdown. Shirtless. Which would be included in the judging.

"Bacon tastes good," said Luca, drawing snickers from the gallery and sneers from the judges with the exception of Sofia, who once again stared him down as if he were standing there naked.

When it came time for me to taste Luca's carbonara—with which he made hand-cut linguini rather than use the pasta maker, I nearly moaned with delight.

No way was I going to win this competition. Luca was just too good.

"If this is predictable, then I don't want to be surprised. Ever," I said.

Corny, yes, but I really was beginning to have fun, and I knew it would make for "good TV."

"The linguini tastes buttery. Comforting. Like . . ."

Like being with Luca back in Alba, riding with him in his car, watching him cook, laughing after pushing him down the hill, biking along the countryside. . . .

"Like being with a good friend," I said, my voice breaking on the last word.

My turn with the judges. Judge Louis smiled encouragingly again and said, "You loosened up out there. I can taste it. I love that you went with prosciutto. And you made a bold choice with the roasted asparagus."

"Thank you," I said, beaming.

"I don't know about *bold*," said Judge Gene, "but at least it wasn't bacon," he remarked as he gave Luca the stink-eye.

"It's good," said Judge Sofia. "Of course you could have grilled the asparagus rather than roasted it just for a little variation from Chef Caramelli's dish. But I guess that's what happens when you're under his influence."

If I didn't know better, I'd have sworn that was code for *banging Luca*, and that she knew he and I had been together last night. Probably was in the room across the hall and heard us. Or down the block, come to think of it.

Judge Louis came to my rescue. "Be that as it may, the Caramellis taught her well." I liked that he used the plural.

"Carbonara isn't really a Genoa thing," I said, remembering Luca's lecture to me in Alba. I could almost see him smile behind me, like a proud mentor. Cass would have been proud as well.

Just as I began to believe that maybe I did have a shot after all, Judge Sofia looked at the dish, then at me. "How would you compare this to your Pasta Pronto carbonara?"

The question stupified me.

"Um . . ." I started. "It's . . . it's different. I mean, there's obviously a difference in taste when you make fresh pasta."

"Which do you think is better?" she asked.

Shit. If I answered, *fresh pasta*, then I'd be publicly admitting my product was inferior, and that would significantly damage the company's reputation, not to mention mine, and the stock. If I answered, *Pasta Pronto*, then I'd be telling a bold-faced lie on television and everybody would know it. Luca would know it. Or worse, if Luca believed I meant it, he'd lose what little respect he had left for me, if any.

"That's a bullshit question."

I whipped my head around to find Luca standing off to the side, staring Judge Sofia down like a guard dog.

Toby shook his head. "*Now* he speaks English," he muttered. "Goddammit."

Judge Sofia gaped at Luca, taken aback. "Excuse me?"

"You can't ask her that," he said.

"It's a perfectly legitimate question," said Judge Sofia.

"Oh, come on," said Judge Louis. "It's a 'gotcha' question."

"Don't you two hate each other?" said Toby, pointing between Luca and me. Luca and I warded off the reflex to exchange glances.

"Look, Katie Cravens is the founder of a highly successful diet pasta line, and she's here, making fresh pasta, and I think her customers want to know what she really thinks," said Judge Sofia.

Judge Gene pointed at me and said, "One look at her tells you which one she's been eating lately."

Holy frappe, did he . . . did he really just take a poke at my weight gain?

Would it be bad sportsmanship if I dumped the carbonara on Judge Gene's head—plate and all—and sucker-punched him in his six-pack abs?

"Excuse me, but you would *never* make such a remark to a *male* contestant," I said. "My body size is none of your business. It has no bearing on the outcome of this competition. It makes no reflection on what I eat or don't eat."

I couldn't stop myself. "*How dare you.* How dare you undermine me and women everywhere by making such a rude, ignorant, irrelevant comment. What does my body size have to do with how that plate of food tastes?" I yelled, pointing at the dish. I turned to Judge Sofia. "And *you*," I pointed. "Where do you get off putting me in a hot seat that serves no purpose but to discredit me regardless of my answer? Which you knew when you asked the question. I have always stood behind what I make. That's all you need to know."

And then, like I hadn't screwed myself with the judges already, I spat out a "Fuck this," and walked off the stage, the camera following me. *The camera following me!* Holy shit, it was all on film! Oh God, what did I just do? What did I just *say*?

The camera operator was still recording my every word and movement. Did the camera capture me shaking with anger and upset and bewilderment? Was it projecting Katie-Cravens-come-undone to the rest of the world? Would Stu Chutney withdraw his offer once he saw how weak I really was?

Wait—that wasn't weakness.

That was strength.

I defended myself. I had every right to.

Not to mention that rather than be mortified by a comment insinuating that I had gained weight and shamefully apologizing for it, I got angry. I spoke out on behalf of my body. Never had I ever done that in my life. My body had never been good enough. Didn't matter what size I fit into. But more alarming, it had never *felt* good enough. These last few months, despite the extra pounds I'd added, I'd also added shape and definition and tone. I added *nourishment*, and not the kind that comes from keeping track of fat and calories and protein levels. I added vitality and pleasure to my life, and my body thanked me for it.

Win or lose *Pasta Wars*, I'd just fought and won a much bigger battle, a war that had been waged against me, by me, throughout most of my life. I knew my life had changed at that moment. But I was just too damn tired—of everything—to acknowledge it.

I faced the camera operator and snarled, "Turn that thing off and get it out of my face right now before I force-feed it to you."

Heather Lawrence appeared and gave the operator the at-ease sign. The operator left us alone. "Katie, that was fantastic," said Heather. "Things had been entirely too friendly until that point. But you can't quit. You're contractually obligated to finish. So why don't you take a little break and cool off, and we'll get things set up for round three."

If that was a pep talk, I may have missed something.

"Whatever," I said. "I'm going to lose this competition anyway. Might as well make my humiliation complete."

She walked away without a response.

I paced about, trying to shake off my anger, fear, frustration. . . .

Luca appeared with a bottle of water and handed it to me. Add "horniness" to the list.

"Maybe we should walk out together," he said. "Can't really do anything to us then."

"I'm not leaving, Luca," I said. "I am not a quitter. And why did you have to say something before? What are you, my knight in shining armor?"

Luca stared at me, incredulous. "You're mad at me because I defended you? Would you rather I'd have let you stand there and incompetently babble on the way you did this morning?"

"I don't need you to fight my battles for me. I don't need you constantly stirring the pot. God, ever since you came into my life, it's been nothing but chaos!"

"You needed chaos, Miss Katie! You needed adventure and passion and fire. You needed to give up some of that false control you so stupidly believe you have."

I lost it again and threw my hands in the air. "Ughhhh!!! I *hate* you, Luca! I hate the way you talk to me. I hate the way

you make me feel. I hate that you make me question everything I've ever believed in. Most of all, I hate that you're *right*.
Just get away from me!" I shouted and stomped off like a fifteen-year-old, lost in the maze of the studio until I found a
restroom, where I cried and splashed cold water on my face
and just stood in front of the mirror, unable to look at myself,
taking deep breaths. So much for fun.

I emerged from the restroom to find John the production
assistant skulking nearby, probably with orders to tackle me
in case I tried to make a prison break.

"You okay, Miss Cravens?" he asked.

I inhaled one final deep breath, and announced, "Let's just
get this over with."

War is hell.

thirty~one

Luca was waiting on the set, leaning against the pasta workstation, awaiting instruction, when I reemerged to applause and even a couple of cheers from the audience, despite their having been instructed to remain silent until the winner was announced. Apparently my telling off the judges had won their favor. I considered apologizing to the judges, but for what? They're the ones who wronged me. No, the person I really wanted to apologize to was Luca. I'd hurt him yet again, when the only thing I'd wanted to do all day was stand close enough to inhale him. What had gotten into me?

The judges wore scowls under their smiles, and I avoided even blinking in their direction. *Just get through this final round*, I told myself. *Remember the one for whom you've been cooking all day.*

Round three was the signature dish. In an actual surprise twist—we weren't even informed of it ahead of time—Toby announced that Luca and I would be sending our finished plates to the judges for a *blind* taste test. I wondered if this was a last-minute change based on the fact that we'd all pretty much pissed one another off, or if this was something Heather Lawrence had been planning to spring on us all along. Either way, the heat in the kitchen just went to inferno level, metaphorically speaking—not only did I have to make Luca's ravioli look like Luca's ravioli, but taste like it too. One final glimpse at Luci before Toby yelled *GO* (we had forty minutes) revealed she was as worried for my fate as I was.

The first time I made ravioli from scratch while prepping for the competition, I'd screwed up royally regarding pasta size and proportions of the filling. Either the pockets broke from being overstuffed, or they weren't stuffed enough, and the shape varied from enormous squares to miniscule rectangles. One even somehow wound up in a sort of rounded triangle.

In truth, Luca had a signature ravioli for each season, Luci had told me. But this one had been voted as a favorite by Caramelli's customers; thus, it had remained on the menu year-round. In other words, "signature" was more of a novelty title than an actual one. Touristy, at best.

We had forty minutes on the clock. I lingered just a step behind Luca, watched him grab three zucchini, and then followed suit. We said nothing as we brushed against each other in our haste to get back to our kitchens.

Because of the last-minute twist, the judges were prohibited from watching us cook so they wouldn't know which was which. Not feeling their hungry, beady little eyes staring at me alleviated some of the pressure; and yet, I blanked out for a split second, just as I had done with the spaghetti, trying to figure out what to do first. I couldn't even sneak a peak in Luca's direction, lest I be accused of copying him. Not only that, but with every passing moment of non-communication, the more crater-like the gap between us became. One look at him reminded me I had already lost.

I worked on the zucchini first, peeling and cutting it up, and then drizzling it with olive oil and seasoning it with salt and pepper to prepare it for the oven. I recalled the recipe saying the zucchini took an hour to roast, so I opted for the convection oven instead, hoping that would solve the time problem. Next, I browned the ground sausage and sautéed the mushrooms and set both aside. I heard Toby comment on Luca's focus, his trance-like state whenever he worked with pasta dough and how precise he was with every cut. To save time, Luca used the pasta maker to roll out the dough, but not to shape or cut the ravioli squares. Pertaining to me, Toby said something in reference to "poor time management," which was pretty funny considering Luca was the one who had the worst time management skills I'd ever seen and I typically scheduled myself down to the nanosecond. Besides, since the disastrous first round, I'd renewed a command of the clock.

After I cranked the dough through the pasta maker, it was time to assemble the ravioli. I checked the zucchini. Done? Not done? I honestly couldn't tell. I mixed the browned sausage and ricotta, added dried parsley and basil and salt and pepper, and tasted. So far, so good. Impatient, I removed the zucchini from the oven, transferred it and the mushrooms to the food processor and pulsed them, then scooped it all into the bowl with the ricotta and the sausage, furiously mixing with a wooden spoon.

If Max could see me now. If my parents could see me now. I'd come a long way from downing Mallomars in one sitting and counting every calorie and avoiding the kind of intimacy that only a well-intentioned, well-cooked meal could provide. I'd come a long way from deprivation.

I tasted. Something was missing.

And then I remembered the scones Luca had made the first time we cooked together in Alba. And the antipasto he made at the villa in Genoa. And the french toast I made for him the night we almost . . .

Nutmeg. *Il sale della vita.*

Luca loved nutmeg.

It hit me: that earthy scent, the one that dichotomously soothed me and made me want to rip off his clothes. The one I'd inhaled all night. It was Luca's scent. He smelled like nutmeg.

And at that moment, another realization became clear: I wanted Luca. Not just in a lick-freshly-whipped-cream-off-his-body way, but something much deeper. I wanted to him to tell me stories about him and Vincenzo—*Nonno*—and playing with pots and pans with Luci when they were kids. I wanted to know the first meal he ever cooked by himself, and for whom he cooked it. I wanted to take long walks with him in Alba, sit across from him at a candlelit table in Trattoria Naturale when no one else was there. I wanted to hold his hand. I wanted to dance cheek to cheek in the dark. I wanted us to hold each other in bed. I wanted to make french toast for him every day for the rest of his life.

I wanted to feed him.

Tears came to my eyes, and I couldn't even use the excuse of chopping onions. I tried to wipe them away with the back of my sleeve, and somehow wound up smearing a spoonful of ravioli filling across my forehead.

Nothing like wearing food on national television to get you to refocus.

I added a dash of nutmeg and tasted. A pinch more and tasted again.

It tasted like Luca.

Using a measuring spoon, I doled out each filling approximately two inches apart from one another, allotting three generous-sized ravioli for each plate, twenty altogether. After that, I brushed the edges with water and carefully overlaid it with the second rolled-out sheet of pasta dough, pressing gently with my fingers between each pocket. Finally, I used the ravioli cutter and perforated each one like a book of postage stamps.

Lo and behold, ravioli.

They cooked in the boiling water quickly.

I tasted one.

Wow.

The sun-dried tomato sauce consisted of garlic cloves, olive oil, a pinch of lemon juice, salt and pepper to season, and fresh basil. I tossed it all in the skillet, and on a whim decided to add a pinch of nutmeg there as well. I didn't know if I would lose points for deviating from the recipe, even so subtly, but maybe the judges wouldn't notice.

What was I saying??? These were foodies of the highest caliber. They'd notice.

For the presentation, I arranged each ravioli triangle style, ladled the sauce on top, sprinkled with a bread crumb and grated parmesan coating, and garnished with whole basil leaves.

My dish looked and smelled beautiful. Plus, I finished with ten seconds to spare.

When Toby called the end of time—and God, he was irking the shit out of me by now—Luca poured two champagne flutes of Prosecco, brought them to my kitchen area, and handed one to me.

With earnest intent, he leaned in close to my ear and whispered, "I'm very proud of you, Miss Katie."

The *kindness* in his voice and words—I didn't deserve it. My insides melted and tears flowed and I completely let go.

"I made it for *you*, not them," I confessed just as softly. "All of it. Every dish."

The look he'd given me in Genoa, the night he'd ended things before they even began, that mix of sadness and fear and being swept away, appeared again.

He clinked my flute with his own, took a sip, and then shook my hand collegially.

thirty~two

Because we were running behind schedule, we barely had time for a break. For the final round Luca and I appeared in front of the judges together, side by side, but first we were filmed tasting each other's food. One taste of Luca's ravioli—bite-sized-friendlier than mine, but so perfectly cut and arranged on a mini-platter, four squares in a line, each slightly overlapping the other—and I knew I'd lost the competition.

Food. Orgasm.

The pasta tasted like silk, yet was the perfect density. The vegetables and cheese and meat and spices were like great jazz, each one listening to and playing off the other, yet also standing alone. I heartily speared and popped the remaining three in my mouth one by one.

Filled me completely.

Luca's turn. He cut one of mine in half, examined it, put it to his nose, and eyed me suspiciously. Then he tasted it.

His expression morphed from puzzlement to wonder to recognition.

"You used nutmeg," he said.

I trembled. "Too much?" I asked. "Or does it clash with the other flavors?"

He simply answered, "It's good."

He was lying. He had to be. Every part of me sagged with disappointment. He didn't like it.

The judges sat in front of our plates: mine marked *A* and Luca's marked *B*.

The Prosecco went right through me. I had to go to the bathroom in the worst way. Between that and nerves, I shifted my weight from side to side.

The judges tasted.

"What is that, nutmeg?" asked Judge Sofia.

Uh-oh.

I hid my face in order to hide any hint in my expression that might give me away. Luca stared at the floor as well, peering up every so often, completely stone-faced. How do people do that?

"It *is* nutmeg," said Judge Louis. "I don't remember ever tasting nutmeg in this dish before, and I'm a major fan of Chef Caramelli's ravioli."

Shit-fritters!

Judge Gene said, "The zucchini filling tastes a little under-cooked to me, but the ravioli is a perfect *al dente*. I like the breading on top as well."

I covered my mouth as if to stifle a yawn or a sneeze, but I wasn't fooling anyone. I knew I was beaming with pride and accomplishment.

Each of them sipped their water, made notes on their scorecards, and pulled Luca's plate in front of them.

Practically in unison, all three of them said, "I don't taste any nutmeg in this one," after each taking a bite.

I shifted from side to side even more frenetically now. Luca remained stony and silent.

"Everything is perfectly cooked," said Judge Sofia. "The flavors go so well together, and there's a sweetness I detect, although I can't tell what it's from."

"I think I'm going to make these for my wife on our anniversary," said Judge Louis. "Or ask whichever of you made this one to come over and make it for me," he said with a chuckle, and eyed Luca for a split second. Luca barely even blinked.

"I'd have to stay at the gym an extra hour because I'd want two servings of this," said Judge Gene.

And just like that, my hopes sank again. But they were right—Luca's ravioli was divine.

The judges cleaned their plates, followed by their palates.

"Miss Cravens," said Judge Louis, "do you think you deserve to win?"

"No," I replied, not even taking time to deliberate.

The judges seemed taken aback by my bluntness, perhaps more used to ego-driven contestants who not only thought they deserved to win, but outright demanded it.

"Why not?"

"Because Luca's food is better."

"You don't think you cooked well?" asked Judge Gene.

"I think I cooked better than I've ever cooked in my life. But that doesn't mean I cooked better than someone who has devoted *his* life to it."

Toby chimed in. "At the *Pasta Wars* press event yesterday, you said you knew 'the secret ingredient.'" He gestured quote marks with his fingers. "Did you use it today?"

I knew what was coming next. If I said yes, they'd make me reveal it.

"I did," I replied.

"What is it?" asked Toby.

A pregnant pause took over. With my peripheral vision, I glanced at Luci in the gallery first, and then lovingly at her brother beside me.

"You'll have to ask Vincenzo Caramelli," I said.

Luca's mouth clamped shut, and he closed his eyes. When he opened them, they were glassy.

"Chef Caramelli, do you know the secret ingredient Katie is referring to?" asked Toby.

He didn't respond.

"Did you use it?" asked Toby.

Still no response. Toby was getting annoyed again, as was everyone else.

"Do you deserve to win?" Judge Louis asked Luca.

"That's up to you to decide," Luca replied.

"Okay," said Toby to Marty. "We're obviously not going to get anywhere with this guy."

Marty told this guy to move on. Toby put on a game show smile and announced, "It's time for the judges to decide the victor of *Pasta Wars*."

Luca and I were supposed to sit together in another room while the judges discussed our dishes, but Luca refused, saying he'd had enough of "the drama." "Just film them scoring the damn things," he said. "You already got their commentary."

Marty, weary with Luca and perhaps with the entire day's filming and production (I could empathize all around), submitted to Luca's demand. But I heard him say to Heather Lawrence, loud enough for Luca to hear, "We're never working with this guy again."

I, however, begged for a bathroom break and ran off the soundstage before being granted permission, my bladder screaming too loudly to care about the laughter from the gallery that followed as I ran off.

When the judges announced that they were finished, Toby took the scorecards and tallied the points. The three criteria for each dish were Presentation, Recipe, and Taste. Ten points was the highest score for each category, zero for the lowest. Thus, a perfect score for each dish would be thirty points; a perfect score for the entire competition would be ninety. I hoped to score at least twenty points for each, knowing my spaghetti dish would probably be the worst.

Of course, this being "reality" television and a competition show, the suspense needed to be dragged out as long as possible. An assistant positioned Luca and me on our marks, facing each other, and once again we had to stare each other down like the superhero and villain (who was which?), but I just couldn't do it. The sweat-induced dampness of Luca's hair sticking out of his bandana. Those sharp cheekbones I had kissed repeatedly the night before. The long, lean body I'd coiled mine around.

All I wanted to do was tell him how sorry I was for everything I'd said and done and stood for. And then kiss him until our lips were swollen.

How in the world had I ended up here? A suburban-kid-turned-MBA-graduate-turned-entrepreneur-turned-CEO, standing on a soundstage at the climax of a cooking competition, face to face with the man I'd slept with twenty-four hours ago. And a pasta troll who hated everything I stood for, a renowned chef who avoided me because I fed him. I'd said the words to him last night, beckoning him to do the same for me without understanding why. I was pretty sure I did now, however.

Did *he* understand? Or did he want to collect his check and get as far away from me as possible?

And what did *I* want? I wanted Luca, but did he want me? And what about where the rest of my life was concerned? What was going to feed me from here on?

Toby stood between us.

"Round one goes to . . ." he paused and shifted his eyes between us before returning to his scorecard for dramatic effect.

It worked. Every muscle in my body tightened as I sucked in a breath and held it.

"Chef Caramelli."

Light applause. No surprise there.

Toby repeated the torture. "Round two goes to . . ."

Again I tensed and inhaled and froze as I awaited Toby saying Luca's name again.

"Katie Cravens."

Louder applause. On the outside, I smiled in appreciation and did a low, inconspicuous fist-pump. On the inside, my stomach did trampoline somersaults.

The tiebreaker.

The defining moment.

One of us would be a winner and the other would be a loser. One of us would be congratulated, and the other would be pitied.

Was it possible I had a shot? Would they give it to me simply because of my personal achievement, like teachers giving students an A for effort? Would they give it to me because Luca was such a pain in the ass? Or was it actually possible that I cooked well enough to rival one of the most renowned pasta chefs in the world?

Well, when I put it that way, it was as far-fetched as it sounded.

Toby fixed his focus on each of us for mere seconds longer than the previous two; and yet, those couple of seconds felt like minutes, hours, months, years, millennia.

"And the winner of *Pasta Wars*—the pasta *champion*—is . . ."

Oh God, kill me now. Make it quick and painless. One blow to the head.

"Katie Cravens!"

Wait, what?

The applause amped up to eleven as I stood there, dazed and dumbstruck.

No. It couldn't be. I won? *I* won???

I expected Luca to erupt into one of his expletive-ravaged tirades, but he just stood there, a quiet, hidden smile threatening to do more than twitch at the corners of his mouth. He took two steps toward me, gently placed his hands on my arms as if to steady me, and kissed me on each cheek, his lips warm and pursed and supple, followed by one on my lips.

And then he walked off the stage without looking back.

thirty~three

I should have been ecstatic. Should have been doing victory dances all over the house, running up stairs with rolling pins to the *Rocky* theme. But all I wanted to do was sleep. My body ached. My neck was stiff. My feet were sore. My appetite was nonexistent. I wondered if the Caramelli twins decided to drive straight to JFK and get on the first plane back to Italy. I wondered if I should have followed them.

I never wanted to see another strip, ring, pocket, or roll of pasta for as long as I lived.

For two hours following my stunning and inexplicable win, the press swarmed me for photo ops and interviews, all arranged by Wendy. All I could think about, however, was a shower. And Luca. Preferably me, Luca, and a shower all at once.

"How does it feel to be the *Pasta Wars* champion, Katie?"

"Do you think Chef Caramelli showed poor sportsmanship by walking off?"

"Will you and the Caramellis still release the new pasta line?"

"Do you think the nutmeg gave you the edge with the ravioli dish?"

"Will Pasta Pronto come out with a low-cal version of that ravioli?"

"Any hard feelings between you and Chef Caramelli?"

Make it stop. Please. Make it all stop.

Pasta Wars filmed on a Friday. I slept until eleven o'clock the following Saturday morning. Then I showered, puttered around the house, and took a nap on the couch for another two hours before finally deciding to just plant my butt there and stream TV shows on Netflix. Max and I use to spend Saturdays bustling around running errands and occasionally taking a one-day staycation in Southampton. I almost always tried to catch up on Pasta Pronto business. But ever since my time in Alba and Genoa, I'd spent the weekends practicing for the competition, keeping the books for Alberto, biking, and even reading for pleasure rather than for work.

Why didn't I follow Luca when he walked off the stage and presumably out of my life? Why didn't I call him, ask him *why* he walked out? Was it bruised ego? Was it all business—he fulfilled his contract, and that was that? Was he really and truly done with me?

I didn't call him for the simple reason that I was tired.

Why didn't he call me?

Monday was business as usual. Except that two more offers to buy Pasta Pronto came in. Apparently Stu Chutney's proposal was leaked to the press following my win. "You can pretty much write your own ticket now," said Marvin, one of my top advisors. "You're the Pasta Queen."

"Next person to call me that gets canned on the spot," I announced. "Without severance."

Marvin cleared his throat. "I'm just saying you have your pick of offers. Or you can stay on as CEO and have fun at the next stockholders meeting. You gotta hand it to Wendy and her team—this was a brilliant ploy from the get-go, and making you win was all the better."

"Wait—what?" I said. "What do you mean, 'making me win'?"

Before Marvin could Maybe-you-should-talk-to-Wendy his way out of it, I buzzed Jennifer to get Wendy's ass in my office *immediatamente*. She made it in five minutes flat. I sent Marvin and the others out.

"Did I win that competition fair and square?" I asked.

Wendy released her spin-smile and, without even pausing for a breath, answered, "You could've served those judges glue and they would've given you the win."

"I don't believe it," I said, before hitting my desk. "I DON'T BELIEVE IT. Did it not occur to you how bad it would look if people knew the thing was rigged? How bad it would look for *me*? It undermines my credibility, the company's, every edge this competition was supposed to give us."

"That's why we didn't tell you. We figured we'd get a more authentic response from you on camera, and we did. It was perfect. You looked so shocked and emotional and grateful."

"And Luca—did he know?"

"We thought it best not to tell him either. Although, frankly, we think maybe he figured it out, given how little of a fight he put up."

"What do you mean? Are you saying he didn't try his best?"

"Well, we were hoping you two would be more . . . combative. After all those quotes we planted . . ."

I stared at her blankly, puzzled. "What quotes?"

For the first time, Wendy looked nervous. "Well, Gianluca had agreed to do the show as a favor to you, but insisted on absolutely no press. We were surprised, given how vocal he'd been in the past, but we figured maybe he didn't want to sour the partnership between you two. So we decided to . . . help things along."

Oh my God, he was telling the truth! He'd never said any of those horrible things. And I . . . I said every single one.

I rose from my desk, circled to the other side of it, and came toe to toe with Wendy.

"Get your ass out of my office, get your team out of my company, and don't ever come back. If you're lucky, I won't sue you."

The color drained from Wendy's face. "You can't be serious."

"Do you want to find out how serious I am?"

"This is the thanks I get for saving your company?"

"*Saving* my company? You put it in jeopardy! You made me look like a fool. Now get out of my office before I have you thrown out."

Wendy, looking like a cheerleader denied the Prom Queen title, skulked off, leaving me there to bubble and stew in my anger, betrayal, and guilt.

All those things I'd said about Luca. All those things I'd believed. After working so hard to try to win honestly, and believing for a moment that I actually did . . .

Who was I kidding? I didn't believe it for a second.

I phoned Luca, and the call went straight to voice mail. Probably saw my name on the caller ID. Or maybe he was en route back to Italy.

"I know it was rigged," I said to the voice mail. "I know you didn't say those things. I'm sorry I didn't believe you. I'm sorry for being a fool and playing right into it. I'm sorry you had to go through that entire charade. Just tell me you gave it your best effort. Tell me you didn't let me win too."

And please don't delete the message, I thought.

I sank in my chair, swiveled around to face the window, and stared at the skyline. I ignored calls from my assistant. I ignored her when she knocked twice and entered my office and said my name. I ignored Siri reminding me about my next meeting.

If word got out—and in this day and age, it was surely going to get out—then what would be the best course of action? Would it be to resign from Pasta Pronto? Was it that serious? I'd refused to even consider resignation during the health scandal. Why was it a viable option now?

Because I wanted to go.

I finally looked at my watch to discover that two hours had passed. Feeling a strange calm, the kind that comes after a storm has ravaged a town or eroded a beach, I buzzed my assistant. "Call Stu Chutney. We're accepting his offer."

I was about to call Luci to inform her about my decision and discuss the fate of our pasta line when my phone pinged.

I didn't know it was rigged. And I did my best. You deserved to win

I texted back:

Tell me what "You feed me" means. Please

No response.
I was done with Luca Caramelli too.

thirty~four

In a world of coconut lovers and coconut haters, pasta buyers and pasta makers, chocolate eaters and chocolate addicts, pantsers and planners, I was a coconut-hating, chocolate-devouring, pasta-making, uber-planning, soon-to-be-former CEO of a successful food company. But all I really wanted to be was Katie Cravens.

Feeling emotionally hungover from the day, I crawled into bed around ten o'clock that night and turned out the light. I was about to silence my phone when it startled me with a ping.

Can we talk?

Luca.

I considered being snarky and replying, *I don't know, can we?* Or just putting the phone back on the bedside table and letting him suffer with no reply the way I did. But I knew me. I'd get no sleep knowing he wanted to talk. And I should at least get some kind of closure with him, right? *Right?*

I typed:

OK

Seconds later:

Good. Let me in

At that moment, the doorbell rang.

Holy frappe, Luca was *here*? At my house?

I cascaded down the stairs to the front door. When I opened it, Luca stood before me, dressed in jeans, T-shirt, and leather jacket—and oh, my God, did he look hot—and holding a bouquet of red roses.

And there I was, wearing zebra-striped silk pajamas.

I gawked at him, his jacket, the roses . . . as if memorizing the image.

"Are you going to let me in, Miss Katie? It's a little chilly out here."

"Oh. Yes. Sure," I said, snapping out of my trance and taking a few steps back. "Come in." He entered, and I closed the door behind us. "How did you know where I live?"

"My sister gave me the address." He extended the flowers. "For you."

I cradled them. "Thank you. They're beautiful."

We stood like statues in the foyer, uncertain who was to speak first or what was to be said.

Finally, I did. "Why?"

"Why, what?"

"Why are you here, Luca? What do you want?" I sounded more suspicious and accusatory than I had intended.

He seemed to consider turning on his heel and taking off without a word, just like he'd done on the *Pasta Wars* set, but instead he asked, "Where's your kitchen?"

I led him to it and turned on the light.

He conducted a panorama viewing before concluding, "This is one of the most depressing kitchens I have ever seen."

"Gee, thanks. You're a swell houseguest."

"The kitchen should be the heartbeat of the house," he said.

"Well, my heart's been broken repeatedly, so . . ."

I opened a cabinet to retrieve a vase for the flowers while Luca opened my fridge and pantry doors. He *tsk-tsk*ed. "Even more depressing. Where is all your food?"

"I run a multi-million-dollar company in Manhattan, not to mention I've been working my ass off trying to beat your ass"—*and a mighty fine ass it is*—"in a competition that was rigged from the start. I haven't had time for grocery shopping."

He ignored me and continued to snoop.

"Do you always just walk into people's houses and peruse their pantries without permission?" I asked.

"Nope. Just yours. Good. You have berries." Along with a bowl of raspberries, he took a carton of eggs and a bag of flour. "At least you have the basics. I brought reinforcements just in case." From the pocket of his jacket manifested a jar of Nutella, like a magic trick. He then opened the fridge again, spied around, and pulled out a bottle of vanilla hazelnut coffee creamer. "This'll do," he said more to himself than to me.

"Luca, it's after ten. What are you doing?"

"What do you think?" He opened cabinets and drawers in search of mixing bowls and utensils.

I helped him along. "If you're making pasta, forget it. I never wanna see or taste it ever again."

"You won't say that after you've tasted this."

I sat on the stool at the island, lazily propped my chin onto my hands, elbows on the graphite countertop, and watched him begin the steps I could now do in my sleep. Flour well. Eggs. Pinch of salt. Oil. Mix. He kneaded and smoothed the dough in no time, and covered it with plastic wrap. Next, he pulled out a saucepan and dumped the raspberries in, added sugar, and turned on the burner.

"You wouldn't happen to have a lemon, would you?"

I shrugged. "Fresh out."

He shook his head as if it were the most sorrowful news he'd ever heard. "*Troppo male*," he said.

He lightly stirred the berries.

"I ·know you've been doing the books for Alberto," he said, the words nearly giving me whiplash from their sudden impact.

I sat up straight, feeling like I'd just been caught embezzling. "I—what—how . . . ?"

He laughed. "You will never make a career as a secret agent," he said.

"Well, there goes my application to secret agent school," I retorted. "Seriously, Luca, how did you find out?"

"I knew somebody was overseeing things when the computer and the software arrived. Then when he started talking cost margins and cutting back on expenditures, well . . ."

He handed me the jar of Nutella and instructed me to spoon it into a bowl. I gave him a dirty look, as if to say, *I'm not your slave*, but those hypnotic obsidian eyes responded with *So, what else is new?* and, as if robotically programmed, I found myself doing what he asked.

"Turns out Alberto has as good of a poker face as you do, so when I asked him about it, he confessed like it was some kind of police interrogation."

I ran a finger along the Nutella-coated spoon and licked the residuals. "How long have you known?"

"Long enough."

"You mad?"

He shrugged. "Why didn't you tell me?"

"Because I thought you would be mad."

He shrugged again and stirred the berries before reducing the heat of the burner. He then poured half the coffee creamer into a small bowl, added a spoonful of flour, and blended the two before adding it to the berries, which intensified the already sweet scent. "I don't know how much longer I'll be there," he said.

"Luci said you'd get bored with it and move on to something else. She thinks you're too flighty."

"Luci is a creature of habit. I'm not. Just because we're twins doesn't mean we have to be the same. And she's wrong. It's not that I get bored. It's that I've been looking for something to fill me since . . . " He trailed off, "I love everything about that place. I love what we've done. And I love Alberto like a brother. I want to stay there. But I think maybe I belong somewhere else." He kept his focus on the bowl. "On second thought, don't heat that up," he said of the Nutella. "Let's work on the dough."

"*You* can work on it," I said. "I'm retired."

He grinned and removed the dough from the freezer. "Your food was really good the other day, Miss Katie. I would never lie about that. You earned that win."

"I can't believe they rigged it," I said, anger whirling inside me like a dust cloud. "And although it's nice of you to say, you can't honestly think my food was better than yours."

"Your ravioli was definitely better. You remembered the nutmeg."

"And here I thought I'd done something original."

"It was original, in a way. It's never mentioned in the recipes. One of my 'secret' ingredients. You used your instinct."

"I'm surprised you left it out."

"I wasn't at my best that day," he said. "Not because I wasn't trying. I was just . . . distracted. You have a way of throwing me off my game."

I failed to suppress a smile. So did he.

"Speaking of which . . ." he started, "where is your nutmeg?"

"I don't think I have any," I said.

Finally, the familiar Luca outrage surfaced. "Have you learned *nothing*? Have I taught you *nothing*? HOW CAN YOU NOT HAVE NUTMEG?" And then came the Italian swearing. I loved every minute of it.

"I have cinnamon," I offered.

"You make it sound like they're the same thing."

"Fraternal twins?"

"Hardly." He exhaled an exasperated sigh. "It will have to do, although this dish is now going to be second rate. Your fault."

"I take full responsibility for its awfulness," I said. He eyed me, and we mutually recognized the moment of playfulness. He added a pinch of cinnamon to the raspberries.

I set up my pasta maker and a saucepan of water, and Luca rolled out the dough. First, he spread pats of Nutella on the dough, inches apart, indicating where the ravioli squares would be cut, and finally the vision was coming together for me. Second, he spooned the berry-and-creamer mixture on top of the Nutella spread, covered it with another layer of dough, and cut it into squares.

"I don't think I've ever eaten ravioli as a dessert before," I said. Luca didn't respond, too engrossed in his work. However, I gasped when he dumped a heaping handful of sugar in the boiling water. "Um, Luca, that's *sugar*, not salt!"

"You think I don't know what I'm doing?" he said, sounding insulted.

"Well, you know, you just said you get distracted around me, so . . ."

"Not *that* distracted."

"Fine," I said, almost disappointed.

He pointed to the bowl of Nutella. "Nuke that, please." I did so, and stirred it when it was done. Luca fetched two plates and set them side by side. Minutes later, he removed the ravioli squares one by one and let them sit for a moment to dry. They looked pillow-soft. He placed two in each plate and drizzled the remaining liquid from the berries onto each, followed by the warmed Nutella. Then he sifted powdered sugar over the top.

"You should have mint leaves." He sighed dramatically. "No nutmeg, no cream, no lemon, and no mint. It's a wonder you've survived all these years without me."

Something about the way he said this sent an electric current up my spine, followed by a pang of longing.

"Luca," I started, "I'm really sorry about all those things I said. I—"

Before I could continue, Luca put a berry-scented finger to my lips to silence me.

"Shhhh," he said with the sexiest pursed lips ever. I opened mine ever so slightly in a tease, allowing him to insert his finger just as teasingly, until he remembered himself and withdrew it, never once disconnecting his gaze from mine.

He cut into a ravioli square with the fork tines, revealing the chocolate-infused berries and cream, speared one half, and held it to my lips, a protective hand underneath the fork to catch any drippings. "Taste *this* instead."

He fed it to me. I closed my eyes.

I proceeded to experience the most intense food orgasm of my life, moaning and uttering *Oh my God* as I chewed.

"Not bad for coffee creamer, eh?" he bragged.

"And to think this is the shit version without the nutmeg and the mint."

I took the fork, speared the other half, and fed Luca in return. He nodded. "Not bad," he repeated. We continued taking turns feeding each other the remaining dessert. Every bite sent me into another frenzy, which I could tell pleased Luca.

Hungry and horny for even more, I leaned into Luca and purred. "Now what shall we do with the rest of this Nutella?"

Luca kissed me hard and tried to lift me onto the island, but this time he had difficulty.

"I'm a fatty now," I said matter-of-factly.

He shook his head and said softly, "No. You're perfect."

I *felt* perfect. I kissed him even harder, pulling him as close to my perfectly imperfect body as possible, breathing in his earthy nutmeg scent.

He stopped and held me tight and nuzzled into my neck. I stroked his hair. He picked up his head and revealed tears in his eyes. "Nonno and I used to spend hours together talking about the wonders of the world and simplicity and love. Shortly before he died, he told me, 'Marry a woman who feeds you in every way. And you must feed her too. In every way.' I told him I would only marry a woman with his blessing. I thought he was going to live forever, you know? I never thought . . ." His voice broke.

I caressed his cheek with the back of my hand.

Luca took a breath and continued. "My grandfather was my world. He was my life. He taught me everything—*everything*. He promised he'd be with me always."

"He *has* been with you," I said. "All this time."

Luca shook his head like an obstinate child. "Not the way I wanted. My heart broke so badly when he died. My life fell apart. I made something of myself just to make him proud, but I knew that all the restaurants and the attention weren't what he really wanted for me. He wanted love for me. But it was too painful. So I closed myself to it. And without his blessing, what point was there to find a woman who fed me when I knew I couldn't feed her back? It hurt too much to go on loving without him there. It hurt to not have his blessing."

He took my hands in his, and stroked them with his thumbs. "When I met you, a fire lit inside me. I couldn't understand it. I have cooked for thousands of people, and a dozen lovers. But cooking for *you*, *with* you . . . it was like cooking with Nonno. It was like he was there, whispering to me."

My heart melted like butter with every tender word.

"And that night . . ."—I knew all too well to which night he referred—"to open my heart so much, for the first time since . . . to know you were the one . . . I just couldn't."

I didn't even realize I'd been crying until he caressed a tear away. "I'm sorry, *mia bella*. I'm so sorry."

A cloud lifted from my heart and soul, as if Luca was apologizing not only for himself, but also for Max, my parents, anyone and anything that had ever hurt me, misrepresented themselves to me, or withheld from me. As if deprivation dissolved like wine reduced in a sauce. I felt free. Light. Open.

"Luca." I breathed. But I couldn't seem to find the words.

"When the competition ended and you said you cooked just for me . . . when you said you knew the secret ingredient. . . ."

"*Love*," I replied.

"Yes," he said. "*Love*. That's when I knew it was time for me to stop being so foolish. Nonno wanted love for me. He sent you to me. I'm sure of it. He sent you to me because he knew I never would have looked for you on my own."

A thought struck me. "You know, I hate to say it, but if it hadn't been for coconut and contaminated product, none of this would have happened. Well, that, and Max being a complete dick."

Luca smiled. "Nah. Nonno would have found a way. And not one that would have made all those people sick."

"So that wasn't Nonno's fault?"

"No, that one's on you," said Luca. I cursed at him in Italian. We kissed for an eternity.

He put his forehead to mine. "Feed me, Miss Katie Cravens. Feed me for the rest of our lives."

I nodded. "I will, Luca. Only if you feed me too."

"Always," he promised. He helped me off the island to escort me up the stairs and into my bedroom. But first he pulled one more thing from his jacket pocket. "Looks like I won't need my guilty pleasure anymore," he said, revealing a Reese's peanut butter cup, and placed it on the island. Just steps from exiting the kitchen, he turned and retrieved the confection. "On second thought, there are two of them. We can share."

ACKNOWLEDGMENTS

Immense gratitude to and for the following:

Jordan Hamessley, Marshall Lewy, and everyone at Adaptive Studios for this fun and terrific opportunity. Thank you for believing in me.

Robert Meitus, for providing excellent counsel, as always.

Sarah Girrell, who assured me this was an authentic Elisa Lorello novel, talked out ideas and offered valuable insight into both the story and characters, and continues to love me despite my disdain for olives.

My cousins Andrew and Daniel Mottola, who provided inspiration one February day, and Gregory Mottola, a.k.a. "The Pasta Troll." Luca would love to have you over for dinner sometime.

My twin brother, Paul, and Kim, his bride, for the awesome birthday present—a pasta maker. The first batch of pasta Paul and I made together is still the best I've ever eaten.

The Undeletables, just because.

My patient, loyal readers.

ACKNOWLEDGMENTS

My mother, Rev. Eda Lorello; my father, Michael J. Lorello; my siblings, nieces and nephews, and their spouses. I love you dearly.

My grandnephew, Kaden, who enthusiastically ate every strand of spaghetti I made.

My in-laws-to-be, Leslie and Charles Clines and Ron Lancaster. *Buon Appetito!*

Most of all, to Craig Lancaster, who feeds me in every way. I love you infinitely.

ABOUT THE AUTHOR

Elisa Lorello was born and raised on Long Island, the youngest of seven children. She earned her bachelor's and master's degrees from the University of Massachusetts-Dartmouth and taught rhetoric and writing for over ten years. In 2012, she became a full-time novelist.

Elisa is the author of the Kindle bestselling novels *Faking It*, *Ordinary World*, *She Has Your Eyes*, *Why I Love Singlehood* (co-authored with Sarah Girrell), and *Adulation*. In 2013, she published a memoir titled *Friends of Mine: Thirty Years in the Life of a Duran Duran Fan*.

Elisa has been featured in the *Charlotte Observer* and the *Raleigh News & Observer*, and was a guest speaker at the Triangle Area Freelancers 2012 and 2014 Write Now! conferences. She continues to write, speak, and teach about her hybrid publishing experiences, and topics in the craft of writing and revision.

Elisa enjoys hanging out in coffee shops, Pop-Tarts and Nutella, reading, and all things Duran Duran. She plays guitar rather badly and occasionally draws.

Elisa has lived in Massachusetts, North Carolina, and New York. She currently lives in Montana with her husband-to-be and also best-selling author, Craig Lancaster.